QUEST FOR A KELPIE

QUEST FOR A KELPIE

Frances Hendry

CANONGATE

First published in 1986
by Canongate Publishing Limited
17 Jeffrey Street,
Edinburgh, Scotland.

Cover illustration by Alan Herriot
British Library Cataloguing in Publication Data
Hendry, Frances
Quest for a kelpie
I. Title
823'. 914 [J] P27
ISBN 0 86241 128 9

Typeset by
E.U.S.P.B., 48 Pleasance Edinburgh EH8 9TJ.

Printed and bound in Great Britain
by Billing & Sons Limited, Worcester.

CONTENTS

Letter to my great-great-granddaughter

*Having attended yesterday a funeral and two birthdays,
I begin, for the first time in my life, to feel old. Perhaps not
before time.*

*The funeral was that of my oldest friend, Celia
Drummond – and a shabby affair it was; only five carriages.
I did not go out to the grave, of course, but at the luncheon
table I told my dear grandson Hector, who had escorted
me, that if he thought to send me off in such poor fashion
I should feel obliged to return from the grave and haunt
him. We could not but laugh, which caused a fine tut-tutting
and head-shaking among the old tabbies. I was remarking
to Hector that dear Celia, if she had been present, would
have been the first to laugh, when I suddenly realised that
I was at least as old as any there. Dear Hector, seeing my
startlement, asked the cause; he looked at me kindly, and
said, "Only in years, Grandmama, only in years." Which
did not cheer me as it was meant to.*

*On returning home, I found a message that my first
great-great-grandchild had made her appearance at about
eleven o'clock. Her father had not informed me earlier
lest I should fret about the well-being of his wife, he said;
though I cannot imagine why I should do so, since she is
as healthy as a Clydesdale horse, and of much the same figure. More like, he feared I should insist on taking charge;
which, on consideration, I must admit was possible. Of*

course, I sent dear Agnes a message of all that was polite, and a basket of the cakes she obviously enjoys so much, which my cook makes better than hers. I said that I should not call until Agnes should be quite recovered, which I've no doubt relieved both their minds, and asked that as a favour to me, the child might bear Celia as one of her names. As James is not one of my known favourites, I feel certain that poor Celia will have this small remembrance.

I then lay down to rest, to prepare for the party which Hector had arranged for me as a surprise for my own birthday; for yesterday I reached my three-score years and ten.

It was a fine gathering. Sixty-seven of my direct descendants – they could not all be present, of course, but there were messages and gifts from the boys in the Mediterranean Squadron and the Fusiliers, and from my grandchildren in Barbados and Pondicherry – which is in India; how Hector arranged it all I cannot imagine; and with their wives, husbands, and one or two friends, we sat down a hundred and eighteen to dinner. A shocking squeeze, but most gratifying.

I wore black, of course – nothing else would be suitable for a lady of my age, though I must admit to a mad desire to wear scarlet, to see their faces. But I could not allow myself the pleasure. However, I had a fine silk taffety, figured, with Mechline lace and a full skirt over six petti-coats; none of this going about in my shift for me, especially in Edinburgh, in October. Some of the girls were frankly indecent, though none is foolish enough to follow the London fashion, which I'm told is to damp their fine cottons to make them cling to the figure. A surer way of catching lung fever I've not heard of – though it must be vastly interesting. However, that's by the way.

In the midst of dinner – far better than poor Celia's, naturally, since the cause of it was alive and present – the talk swung to discussion of the plans of the French Emperor Napoleon to invade England. When I declared that he was welcome to do so, they all pooh-poohed me, and were in a fine fury of patriotism, with great expressions of hatred for the Corsican Tyrant, and drinking Confusion to the French. My mind went back to my own childhood, when there was another invasion, and equal fervour on both sides; and I realised, once again, that it takes little to stir people to passion.

And then another thought struck me, which shocked me beyond words; I looked at all these noisy, cheering people, my own children and their children, and knew that there was not one of them that I either liked or respected. Even Hector, my favourite, is merely the best of them.

I love them, of course; it is one's Christian duty to love one's family. But I should not, given the choice, have chosen any one of them as a friend. My children are incredibly boring and stuffy – which I'll swear they did not inherit from me – my genteel grand-children disapprove of me, and my namby-pamby, niminy-piminy great-grandchildren are afraid of me. If they did not hope to inherit from me, not a one of them would have bothered to come celebrate my birthday.

I sat, and listened, and smiled, and said little, and thought my own thoughts. It could just be an old woman's fancy that the men seemed pompous and weak, the boys stupid and thoughtless, and the women vain, shrill and useless, in comparison with the folk of my youth; but I think not. Perhaps it is simply that they have never known, any of them, real hardship, which makes folk mature.

So I thanked them prettily, for their faults are not their fault, maybe, drank off my brandy – which I'll swear they'd watered, drat them – and came away early to my bed. They could laugh at me if they chose, and dance that shocking new dance, the waltz – actually holding your partner, how indecent – I must learn it soon – and wonder how much longer I should last, poor old soul, and whether I should re-member this one or that in my will.

While I lay and remembered – none of them.

And so. my dear little new great-great-granddaughter Celia, I shall write this tale for you, not for any of them. It will be kept for you, with my pearls, for your twelfth birthday present. It is the story of the great adventure I had when I was about that age. I shall write it in English, for I fear your mother will not allow you to learn either of the good Scotch tongues of my day, and I shall try to be accurate; but if my pen or my memory slips, pray forgive me,

It comes to you with all the love I fear I shall not be there to give you in person; and I trust you will like me as I was then, as I hope I should like you as you will be.

4

THE FIGHT

It began, as far as I was concerned, with the fight.

At midday one Friday, about the beginning of September, 1743, a month before my tenth birthday, my mother called me in. As there had been no fishing for a week because of storms, there was no fish to take up the country, and I had a bit leisure to play with my little brother Isaac and the twins. Not Ellen, of course. She had her own friends, always.

"Come in, Jeannie," mam called. "Away over with your dad's bite. You can take the wee one with you, an' be sure he takes no harm. Now mind an' dinna spill it, or I'll skelp you."

"Aye, mam," I said. I knew fine she wouldn't – if anybody skelped me it would be my dad. But it was a nuisance having to take Isaac. At near three, he was big enough to be into everything, but too wee to know what to keep out of. Oh, well, at least I didn't have to take the twins, or the new baby.

I tied Isaac's lead rope round my waist to leave my hands free.

"Goin' out a walk, Jeannie?" he yelled in my ear as I fastened it round his shirt under his arms.

"Aye," I said, "an' dinna you pull at me, mind." He grinned again. We both knew he would. Gingerly I picked up the wooden bowl of broth, and lifted a corner of the cloth to sniff.

"Hurry now, afore it gets cold," mam said. "You'll get

yours when you're back. Here, Isaac, you can carry the heel o' the loaf. Go canny, now." With luck, that would calm him down a bit, and dad would get most of the soup.

The twins smiled at us as usual as we went out. For once, Isaac walked carefully as he'd been told – but talking nineteen to the dozen. I whistled as we went, now that I was out of gran's hearing.

Past the broken houses, where the fishers had taken their roof timbers when they left, we scrunched down over the stones to the first big dune. I saw a score of figures in the whins on the far side of the river. The gipsies were back, at their big winter campsite near the Kingsteps quarries. The year must be growing late.

We trudged round the end of the drift that had turned the river away from the town before I was born. The best harbour now lay away towards Lochloy, near a mile east, on Brodie of Brodie's land, and many of the boats and their men had moved there. The six or seven that were left were lying on the sand at the back of the bigger, sea-side dune, by the small lagoon trapped there. They were safe from any storm there, though it was a long haul up from the water's edge.

My dad's four-oar coble was the biggest and best. It was right up out of the water, upside down. Duggie Ralph, who rowed beside dad, was watching a small fire beside it, where a big pot was heating.

"What's he doin', Jeannie?" asked Isaac.

"Tarrin' the boat," I said.

"What for?"

"To keep the water out."

Like every other child, I altered course to avoid Duggie.

"Want to see, Jeannie," Isaac insisted, tugging at the rope.

"Watch out, you daft wee neep!" I said, as the soup jappled in the bowl. "We'll maybe see on the way back. Mind dad's bread, now!" He argued, but I paid no heed, and we tramped on through the soft sand to where dad and the rest of the men were arguing.

One of the other boats had some rotten strakes, and they

6

were knocking them out and cutting new ones to replace them. It was a fiddly job, and they were all in a fine temper. Ten days they'd been cooped in by storms, and now the fine weather had come back on a Friday – and no-one would risk disaster by going out first on the unluckiest day of the week. So they were all frustrated and on edge – but dad turned to us with a smile as usual.

"Well, now, if it's no' my big girl, an' my big boy, eh? What's this? My bite? Well, who's a clever loon to carry it ower without droppin' it! And broth too, eh? No' a drop spilled. That's fine, just what I needed."

Dad could always make you feel that what you did was valuable. He sat down by us, his broad shoulders and barrel chest all gritty with sand stuck to the sweat.

"Well, now, what's the news?" he asked.

Pleased to be first with it, I said, "The gipsies are back, dad."

He looked surprised. " What? Already?"

"There's some o' them comin' across the ford now," I said. Everybody looked. Sure enough, two figures were walking round the first dune. A boy and a girl.

"Thievin' tinks!" growled a voice.

"Now, Davie," dad said quietly.

"They're early this year," said my cousin Donnie. "A hard winter comin', maybe."

"Speakin' from experience, eh?" Jaikie Mackenzie, the fourth man in dad's boat, broke in with a grin.

I watched with interest as Donnie blushed – even his ears. Although at sixteen he had done a man's work for years on the boat, he was still shy, and went even redder as the daffing spread through the group and the men relaxed.

Several other children and wives had arrived, with bowls and baskets. A couple of lads started a friendly tussle in the sliding sand, and somebody got a spray of sand in his meat. There was a shout and a couple of clipped ears, and dad handed the bowl back, empty.

"That was grand, Jean. Say thanks to your mam for me.

7

Now off you go an' leave us get on, or Kennie's boatie'll no' be ready for the New Year, let alone the tide the morn." Without waiting to see us go, he turned back to his work. "Look, Kennie. That bittie there'll have to come out as well, or we're just wastin' our time. You canna fix sound wood on done wood an' expect it to last. It'll come in on you with the first big wave." And the arguments started again.

Kennie always tried to skimp a job. He never scraped his boat – dad said he didn't dare, it was just the barnacles held it together.

"Come on, Jeannie!" Isaac tugged on the rope. He had his wee eyes fixed on the driftwood fire. To humour him, I moved over, away from the rest, to where Duggie sat alone as usual. None of the men liked him, though he was a strong, reliable worker. Not even my dad, who liked most folk, and rowed beside him. Mam avoided him. Some of the women didn't, though they tried to hide it; for he was fine and handsome, well over six feet, with curly fair hair and beard. We children were warily polite to him, and kept out of his long reach. But with dad only thirty feet away...

"Comin' to speak to me, eh?" he said sourly. "I'm honoured."

I didn't know what to say, so I said nothing, my eyes on the big pot perched on three stones above the hot glow. Isaac moved towards it, and reached out to touch it. Duggie was right by, and I expected him to put his hand out to stop Isaac, but he just sat and watched him with a half-smile. I pulled the rope and jerked the wee one back just in time. "Aye," Duggie smiled, "you'll need to watch him close, Jeannie. He'll get hurted some day if you dinna mind him." Aye, and no thanks to you if he didna, I thought, shocked.

Suddenly I heard a foot on the gravel beside me. The gipsy girl stood there, about thirteen or fourteen. She had silver earrings. I gazed fascinated at them gleaming through her black ringlets.

Duggie scowled. "What dae ye want?" he snarled. "There's naethin' here worth the stealin'."

The girl's olive skin flushed slightly under the dirt. "Ach, I wasna for stealin' anythin' at a'," she protested.

"Well, it'll be the first time ever," Duggie jeered at her.

Isaac was still trying to get at the pot, and she knelt down beside him and lifted him away. As he squirmed to get out of her arms, I stepped forward protectively, but then, surprisingly, he turned his head quickly and gave her a kiss on the cheek. She looked near as taken aback as I was myself, but she laughed, and kissed him in return.

Duggie was not pleased. "Put that bairn down and clear out of here," he ordered her. "We dinna want any o' you tinkies round. What d'ye want, anyway?"

"Hae ye a droppie tar to spare?" she asked.

"Tar? That's a new ane."

"The garron's gone lame, and the old man says the pine resin'll no' dae this time," she said. I could hear the professional gipsy whine coming in her voice now. "We'll pay if ye canna spare it."

For a moment I thought that the insult she had implied, that Duggie was too poor to be able to give away a little tar, had done its work. She thought so too, for she held out an iron pan. Duggie even reached towards the ladle, but then his hand drew back and he laughed. "Na, na, ye'll no' get away with that ane," he said. "Ye can hae your tar, but ye'll have to pay for it."

After a moment she shrugged. "How much?" she asked, and her hand moved into the folds of her ragged plaid.

"I'll tell ye what," he said. "Ye can hae it for naethin'." We all three looked at him in distrust, as his teeth grinned wide and white. "Just a kiss," he said. "Like the bairn. Ye kissed him – weel, kiss me the same, an' ye can hae the fill o' your pannie o' tar."

Well! What would Annie Ralph say if she knew her husband was kissing dirty tinks? I looked around for advice, but my dad and all the other folk were watching the gipsy lad doing handsprings for farthings on the far side of the group. I looked again at the girl. She was pretty – black hair and eyes, and full red lips, and a kind of swing to her that our hard-working, hard-worked lassies seldom had, and soon lost. Poor Annie!

"Kiss ye?" She sounded alarmed – but not very.

"Aye. One wee kiss, that's a'. A bonny quean like you must hae been kissed afore. Come awa', now, ye'll enjoy it." She didn't look as if she'd enjoy it. As he rose, so did she, leaving Isaac standing. "Dae ye no' want your tar? Just a wee kiss an' a cuddle." Here, in front of everybody?

She hesitated, but shook her head and started to turn. He lunged out fast and caught her wrist. She tried to jerk away from his grip. When she failed, she bent her head and set her teeth in his hand, kicking silently, writhing like a snake. He winced, and clouted her across the side of the face with his other hand, hard enough to make her teeth clack. As she fell backwards, he jumped towards her, and his foot caught in the trailing rope that joined Isaac and me. Isaac, dragged off his feet, scraped his knees on the gravel and started to scream. Duggie fell yelling, and twisted sideways to keep out of the fire, but one flailing leg knocked the pot of tar spinning and spilling from the fire to the boat, running a black splash over the dry wood that instantly yellowed with little licking flames.

It all happened in a second. When dad and the rest turned at Isaac's cry, they saw the gipsy girl sprawled in the gravel while Duggie on his knees threw sand on the boat to put out the flames.

It was all clear enough, as he explained it. The gipsy had begged for some tar, and when he refused it had kicked over the pot in spite. The girl, held by two of the men, had tossed her hair down over her face and stood sullenly silent, as she had fought. She answered no questions, as if she knew she would not be believed, or was too proud to explain. The boy had disappeared.

Mutters of anger ran through the group. Sensing a drama, more folk from the houses came running over the dune.

"That damned tinks – worse every year – dae somethin'

– the bailies – ach, they're useless – damned tinkies – thievin' an' burnin' – should burn them – aye, that's it, burn them! Burn them out!"

Whoever said it, it found instant agreement. There were about a hundred folk there now, and the noise mounting. They milled about, shouting, and the dogs starting to bark in excitement.

The girl's head lifted for a moment, and her eyes glinted through her hair, but then she looked down again hopelessly.

"Whit d'ye say to that, eh, my quean?" one wife screamed at her. "Ye'll get some o' your ain back – burnin' our boats, eh? Would ye dare? Here, gie her to me an' Katie, we'll hold her for ye!" It wasn't hold she meant.

"Ye canna let them get awa' with this, John Main!" Duggie Ralph shouted. And my dad finally nodded, and agreed it had to be done.

It was the triumphant sneer on Duggie Ralph's face that forced me into action. I had been brought up not to argue or contradict my elders – and speaking against Duggie Ralph was worse than that. But I couldn't let my dad go on with this. I felt, if I didn't stop dad, Duggie would have beaten him somehow. It just wasn't right.

I untied the rope and told Isaac to hold the bowlie and keep out of folks' way, and then shoved and wriggled between the skirts and legs, my bare toes suffering from hard heels, until I could grasp dad's shirt. He was talking to some of the men, organising a runner to go out to the boats at Lochloy, for he knew there would be a fair number of gipsy men at the big campsite, and they would fight like devils. He would need all the help he could gather. They were saying somebody would get killed for sure, and laughing excitedly.

I tugged at his arm until at last he realised I was there. "On ye go hame, Jeannie, I haena' time for ye just now."

"But dad –"

"Off wi' ye!" he snapped.

"But it's no' true!" I screamed – but he wasn't listening. Someone in the crowd bumped me, and I fell backwards over a dog. I was growing desperate.

"What are ye haverin' about?" Donald dragged me up as dad turned impatiently away to speak to another man. "Awa' tae your mam!"

"But what Duggie said – it's a lie!" I screeched in his ear. At last I had somebody's attention. And my dad turned, hearing the word 'lie' above the din.

"What's a lie? Quiet a minute, Alec. What is it, Jeannie – quick, now!"

I hesitated, suddenly overcome and afraid, as eyes started to turn to me. I saw Duggie's face beginning to twist and redden with anger, and nearly lost my courage. But then the gipsy girl looked up. Her face had a red welt across it where Duggie had hit her, and blood where the women had been scratching. Someone had torn out her earrings. The words rushed out almost in spite of me.

"It was Duggie kicked ower the tar. He said he'd gie her some tar if she'd kiss him, and she wouldna, and so he tried to kiss her anyway, an' fell ower the rope, an' the tar went. It wasna her, it was him." I started to sniff.

The faces turned from me to Duggie.

"She's lyin'. She's a lyin' wee bitch." No-one spoke. "It was the tinkie that done it, no' me." There were more than two hundred there now, and scarce a sound but my sniffs and the gulls crying. A hint of desperation dimmed the temper in his voice. "Would you credit a stupid wee lass instead o' me?"

But they all knew him too well. Yes, some of them did believe me, and others weren't sure.

My dad took me from Donald's arms. He wiped my face with a corner of my apron, set me carefully on my feet, and stepped back, so that I was alone. I looked up at him, and from him to Donald and Jaikie and all the other stern faces. I stood up straight, and tried to stop sniffing and trembling.

"Now, Jeannie, tak' your time. Swear to me, Jeannie, by God Almighty, that what ye said was the truth. Now think – if ye said it just to save the lass there, we'll understan', an' ye'll no' get in bother for a kind thought, but ye must tell us true. By your faith in God, Jeannie – who kicked ower the tar?"

My dad had never spoken to me so seriously before. I could feel Duggie's rage behind me, like a cold wind burning my back. But there was nothing else for it. Now I could only tell the truth, whatever happened.

"It was Duggie. Here's the mark on his hand where she bit him."

That mark, and the fact that he hadn't mentioned it, convinced the last doubters. Duggie stood scarlet with rage and humiliation, as the mutters rose again, but in a different tone.

I pushed over to the gipsy girl. "Are ye a' right?" I asked. The women holding her had slipped away in the crowd. She was rubbing her arms where they had gripped and hit her. Still silent, she glanced at me, then up to what was happening behind me,

"Ye'd hae had us dae murder on innocent men for your lies!" dad was saying in disgust and anger.

"Ach awa', man!" shouted Duggie. "Innocent? They're but tinks! There's no' ane o' them innocent. If they didna do this, they've done worse. Will ye be the next minister? Damn ye an' that red-heided bizzom o' yours – she's aye been unlucky! But what can ye expect if ye wed a Hielan' bitch -"

And my dad hit him.

It was a terrible fight. The whole of the fishers were there, cheering and jeering, and eventually falling silent as they surged round the men, up and down the dunes, in and out of the water. Annie Ralph was there, white and shaking. My mam was there, holding Isaac, jostling and screaming among the rest. Even Ellen was there, on the edges.

At first, I was afraid for dad. Duggie was far bigger, tall, strong, tough, with a long reach and stride. He punched dad from a distance, and the blood spattered wide. But my dad, though eight inches shorter, was not small; he was burly, with huge shoulders from pulling an oar or a rope all his life. And he had sailed when he was young to Rotterdam, Hamburg, and Stockholm, and learned to fight in those fierce cities.

So while Duggie punched at his face, dad caught what blows he could on his arms and shoulders, or ducked his head into them, and that hurt Duggie's hands; and all the time he was thud, thudding at Duggie's stomach and chest.

Gasping, Duggie broke away at one point, and tried to leave. But the crowd would not let him go. He'd lied to them, near got some of them killed. The men, and women too, circled him solidly and drove him back to where dad was gasping too, waiting for him.

He could, and did, fight on. He tried everything he knew. He punched, and he wrestled, and he kicked. He grabbed an oar, and half-stunned my dad, but dad wrenched it away from him and broke it over his back. Once when they were in the waist-deep pool he held dad face down for a year; my heart near stopped, and mam turned linen-white, but at last with a huge splash dad heaved out again and threw him off. Duggie tried for an adze, too, but one of the women kicked it out of reach just in time.

After an age they were both so spent they could scarcely lift an arm, and covered in blood. Most of it was dad's, and his face was an awful sight, but he kept on going; though eventually they were on their knees more than their feet, too tired almost to stand. You could see the huge effort it took dad to carry on, to go on hammering his fists at Duggie, but he would never stop while life was in him; and at last Duggie understood that.

I had once heard a man say he would rather face the wrath of God than John Main when he was roused. Now I saw what he meant.

And in the end, my mam stepped forward and stopped it.

There was a queer stillness as we walked down the hill of sand. Even the dogs fell silent. Nobody spoke; nobody cheered. Only here and there a man said "Ah!" like after a full meal, or a woman gulped. They just opened a space in front of us and we walked through, dad resting one battered hand – and more weight than he'd want anyone to know – on my shoulder, and the blood trickling down my back into my shift; mam quietly supporting him on the other side, and Isaac, shocked to speechlessness for once, holding mam's skirts for comfort.

Even when the Bailies' men arrived, carefully late as usual, and asked dad how he got in this state, and he told them the usual answer, that he'd fallen in the boat – for fisher matters were none of the Town's affair – the normal laughter and jeering were missing. Everyone just stood and watched in an odd, shamefaced way. For this had been no ordinary fight.

Annie knelt alone, sobbing wretchedly over her man's unconscious body. I wondered how she was going to get him home.

THE SIGHT

Gran Main, dad's mother, hadn't come down to the fight, with wee Morag and the twins to see to, but she knew all about it. When we reached home, we found that with rare sense she had put the big pot of water on the fire to heat, and Donnie, who had run home ahead of us, had pulled one of the chaff mattresses off the top of the box bed so that dad could lie straight down in front of the fire.

"What way is this for a God-fearin' man tae go on?" Gran greeted us. "An' you – " to my mam, "- runnin' out an' leavin' the bairn, an' her greetin' for her milk. What'll the minister say, John Main – fightin' like a heathen, an' your child speakin' up in front o' the whole toon as if she wis the Provost – ye should be ashamed o' yoursel', Jean Main, so ye should, an' if ye were mine I'd leather ye – the way ye've been raised ye should ken better. None o' mine would ever ha' made such a display o' theirsels. Morag, will ye sit doon an' feed that bairn before she deafens us? I'll see to my son."

Dad had folded up onto the mattress, while mam sat down wearily on the three-legged creepie stool by the fire. The pride that had brought dad home on his own feet had died down. They were too tired to argue – and besides, they were used to Gran's constant complaints and prayers. Mam took the baby and started to feed her. I set out a bowl of soup for Isaac – it was the only way to keep him quiet –

two for the twins, and one for Ellen, who came in just after us, excited.

"Gran," I suggested, "will you see to Eddie an' wee Donnie? Ellen canna manage them both." She turned, distracted by the needs of the five-year-old twins, her favourites because they needed her most. As mam smiled gratefully at me, Donnie and I took a deep breath and started to do what we could for dad.

Mam told us what to do. Donnie washed off the worst of the blood and sand, while I got out the herb basket from under the bed. Dad had lost three teeth, and more were loose, but they might re-fix themselves if left alone. We boiled water to make poultices of moss and comfrey, for his hands and face.

By this time the baby was quiet, and mam could lay her down. She did what we could not; straightened dad's broken nose and wedged it with rolls of cloth, and laid the poultices so he could still breathe. She checked the deep gash the oar had made in his scalp, but the skull beneath seemed sound, and she tied hairs across to hold the wound closed.

Half-way through, he rolled over and was sick, shaking on the pallet. Ellen and Isaac stared, silent at last. This was not the dad they were used to.

We cleaned up, gave dad some willow-bark and hensbane tea, and found that his jaw was broken, too. Mam was cursing quietly in the Gaelic as she bound it.

"We must just hope it sets straight, Jean. It should, please God. Ye've got most of the sand out of the cuts, well done. An' the blood's near stopped. Now you an' Donnie go an' sup – I'll just rub him warm, and he'll dae."

"Dae, will he?" moaned Gran. "Aye, it's easy seen it's no' your son that's lyin' half dead."

"No, mother, it's my man," mam snapped, sharply. "Be quiet now, and look after the bairns for me. I haena the time to be arguing. Say a prayer for him, if you like."

That was all Gran needed, and her voice rose in pleas to the Almighty to spare her son – mostly, I gathered, so that he could look after her in her old age. As Isaac and Ellen started to fidget, I gave them a bannock each and sent them out to play. The twins, as they always did, just sat and smiled. I lifted them outside the door, tethered them to the doorpost as usual, and left them to sit in the sun and watch the hens scratching.

It seemed strange, that with all that had happened it was still only the afternoon.

Mam was uneasy. It was more than the worry about dad, who had stopped shivering under the blankets and seemed to be asleep. She kept glancing at the door, and rubbing her ear as she did when she was fretting.

"What is it, mam," I asked.

"Where is a'body?" she said. "There's somethin' wrong. That door should be packed wi' folk, comin' to see how is John, an' talk about the fight, an' see can they help, an' tell me how is Duggie Ralph. What is it that they're no' here?" We looked at each other; she was right. It was uncanny, that not a soul had come by.

"Dae they think I did wrong?" I asked. "Mam, dae you think I did wrong?"

"No, no, mo chridh, I heard what you did. Ye had tae. That man's goin' to get somebody killed yet. No, you were right enough. I'm proud o' ye. I wish ye hadna had tae, but – " She sighed, and glanced at dad, lying quiet. "Should I go see if I can help Annie? It's no' her fault. No, I'd best stay away. If he thought she'd asked my help, he'd maybe kill her."

We all knew what she meant. Duggie would take out his defeat on Annie, as he did every setback or ill luck. She couldn't risk making Annie's life even worse.

"Maybe he's dead," I suggested, half hopefully.

"Na'," said Donnie. "He's no' that easy killed."

"He'll hae a couple o' cracked ribs, anyway," mam declared with satisfaction. "That'll maybe learn him – though I doubt it."

"The man's an animal," Gran said.

"Na', he's no'." The voice from our feet made us jump.

"John!" cried mam. "We thought you were sleepin'. How do you feel?"

"That's a damned stupid question, woman," the slurred, difficult voice grunted. "How dae ye think I feel? How am I?"

Mam was half laughing, half crying with relief that he was conscious, and his wits were whole. It was Gran who answered.

"No better than ye deserve, ye- ye Papist!" She could think of nothing worse to call him, the tears running down the wrinkles of her old face. "Ach, what a sight you are – ye'd fright the devil himsel'. Your nose is broke, an' your jaw's broke, and the half o' your teeth are awa' down the beach, an' your face looks like a bait-bucket." True enough – the mass of cuts, black bruises and odd-shaped lumps under the bandages had looked like a pailful of broken mussels ready for the hooks. "Ye'll no' be at the fishin' for a month."

The bandages rolled to the side. "...The morn."

"No, John!" mam protested.

"Duggie'll be there."

"He couldna be," she said.

"Aye, Auntie Morag, he will, though," Donnie said. "He's hard. He'll be there, to prove he's the better man. That's what they were fightin' about. Yon on the shore was just an excuse – its been comin' for months. Aye, Duggie aye thought he should be captain. An' if he'll can go out the morn, an' Uncle John canna – "

"Ye'll no' hae him in your boat still, dad?" I asked, amazed.

"Why no'? I'll be there. He'll no' beat me that way neither."

"But you've just been fightin'!" I said. Dad sighed at having to explain.

"Ach, leave it, Jeannie," said Donnie. "Women just doesna understan' these things. He's a good worker, an' he's needed. There's no' many can pull an oar to match your dad, so that the boatie steers right. If your dad's there, there'll be nae trouble. But if he isna – " He shrugged.

"Well," mam sighed, resigned. "Men! Jean, if your dad's to go out the morn he'll need leeches on those swellings round his eyes, or he'll no' see. You an' Ellen run ower to the quarry pool an' see can ye find me a dozen fresh ones."

"Good lass," dad muttered – and not to me.

When we got back with the pot of leeches – we'd been lucky and found fifteen in an hour, though Ellen had mostly sat on the bank and wailed about the mud squelching in her toes – we ran up from the river into the house to find a deputation. Dad was up into Gran's chair, and the mattress was put away again. Two of the fishermen, old Jamie Bochel and Dugald Main, a cousin of dad's, were standing on the hearth-rug, looking awkward but determined. My mam was blazing angry at them.

"Tell her yoursel's!" she shouted. "Go on, you tell her!"

"What is it, mam?" I said, as nobody spoke. Ellen slid away in a corner.

"They say ye're no' to go down to the boats any more, Jeannie. You've red hair, an' it's unlucky. I never heard such nonsense!"

"Aye," said gran, "there's nothin' mair illchancy near a boat nor a red-headed woman, God kens. I telled ye that when ye were courtin', Johnnie, but ye wouldna listen."

I pulled a plait of my hair over my shoulder and studied it. It hadn't struck me before, but it was certainly red – much redder than mam's warm gold – more like my Granda Mackay's must have been when he was young.

"A red-haired wife – " said Jamie.

"She's no' ten!"

"Old enough," Jamie insisted.

"An' ye canna deny," said Dugald, "things go wrong when she's about. There was that time she got into Charlie Manson's boat, an' he was drowned no' a month after."

"An' she was by when Kennie was bringin' in his coble, an' it slipped, an' broke Kennie's leg."

"Kennie's aye haein' accidents!"

"But she was there." Jamie was embarrassed, but

20

stubborn. And there were a dozen stories more, of how boats I had been near had been overset by basking sharks, or damaged by rock or storm.

"An' now the day," said Jamie.

"Aye," Dugald agreed.

"Now we're no' sayin' she's got the evil eye, Morag – "

"Ye better hadna!" Mam's own eyes seemed to be aflame, but Jamie stuck it out.

"- But she's no' chancy. An' we dinna want her down by the boats again. We had a meetin'," – so that was where everybody had been – "an' we're a' agreed. We're sorry, but there it is. Well?"

"What dae ye mean, well? You've decided. What's it to dae wi' us? Oh, John!" Mam turned to the one person she leaned on. He said nothing.

"Dad?" I didn't know what to do. I couldn't be always unlucky, surely? I touched every boat almost every fishing day, harnessing the pony to them to help haul them in, and they didn't all have accidents. How could they say that? What should I do? "Dad?"

There was a long pause. Then my dad stirred in his chair, and slowly rose to his feet. He peered for me through the slits in the bandages, and beckoned me to him. His big hand on my shoulder for the second time that day, he spoke to them, his voice surprisingly clear.

"Thank you for comin'. It wasna an easy job, I'm thinkin'." They looked, if possible, even more shamefaced. "We dinna believe that Jeannie is unlucky, but if that's what the most of you thinks, we have to attend you. She'll no' go near the boats again. You hear that, Jean?"

"Aye, dad." What else could I say?

"Aye. Well -" he said.

"Aye, we'll hae to be awa'. Good day, John. We're sorry. Mistress Main. Morag." They backed out, as if from royalty.

Dad sat down heavily. Mam ran to him, and took us both in her arms. "Oh, John! Oh, John!" was all she could say.

"My God!" said Donnie, who had been silent all the while.

"Dinna ye take the name o' the Lord in vain, Donald Main," Gran started to scold. "It's the judgement of the Lord on ye, Jean Main – "

"For God's sake, mother, hold your tongue!" dad interrupted. As she gasped in pure shock, he turned painfully to mam. "I'm sorry, wife, but there was nothin' else to dae. We canna go again' them a'. An' if that's how they feel, she's better awa'."

"Oh, John, I ken that. It just makes me wild, that – Well, it just means she'll no' be a fisher wife after all. Never you fret, pettie," mam said consolingly, but her hands were shaking. "We'll find somethin' better for ye. Dinna you care for what they say. Ye're no' illchancy. They're a' fools."

She hugged me hard. "Mind the leeches, mam, you'll hae them a' ower the floor," I protested, and at that she began to cry. Dad clumsily put his bandaged hands round her shoulders, and gently held her to him.

As Gran opened her mouth, Donnie and I glared at her, and she shut it again and went out in blessed silence to see to the bairns. Ellen slipped out too. She had a fine lot to tell her friends that day.

All the rest of the day I felt lost. I couldn't really be illchancy? I knew the unlucky things – using the word church, instead of bell-house, or letting our cockerel out of his basket to be seen by the men on their way out. Was I like that? And if I couldn't go to the boats, what would I do? I brought in peat, fetched water from the river, changed the twins' cloths, and all the time my thoughts went round and round like a squirrel in a basket. What would I do? What would I do?

Ellen played and whispered with her friends, as they all went out to gather the mussels for the bait, but no-one would speak to me. I felt like a ghost.

When Johnnie came in from the school, very proud of his dad – they'd heard all about it – he wanted me to describe

22

the fight, and we near came to blows ourselves because I couldn't put my mind to it. He didn't understand how I felt about the ban they'd put on me.

"Lucky for you!" was his comment, his round red face grinning at me. "Dae ye want to spend your life up to the elbows in fish guts? I'll no' dae't, that's for sure. Why dae ye think I'm stickin' in at the school? Auld Rosy Nosy's the dullest thing on twa feet, but it's better than the fishin'. What're ye complainin' about?"

Ellen finally gave him the story he wanted, and they and Gran went over and over it while we baited the lines for the morn, until I could have cried with rage.

Dad stiffened as the day wore on, and it worried him. By evening his arms would barely move, for all his determination. Mam lowered the swelling round his eyes with the leeches, and put on more salve and hot cloths, but that was all she could do, though she was skilly.

As night fell, we took down the mattresses and put the wee ones down to sleep. Johnnie went and brought in Dancer, our pony, the only one in the fisher town, and put him ben the house in the stall, and called the pig in from rootling in the middens to be fed and penned in beside him. We fed the hens, and they settled to roost in the rafters. Ellen, just seven, was away to our pallet in my gran's cubby behind the fire, and Johnnie was just slipping in with Isaac when there was a tap at the door, and the sound of running feet.

But when I opened the door, there was no-one there. Just a pair of silver earrings on the step.

Even now, in the pitchy dark, that momentous day was not over. Mam and Donnie were discussing who could have brought them to us, while dad grunted "Uhuh" occasionally, when we heard a scratch at the door.

"What now?" said mam, between exasperation and fear. She marched to the door, swung up the bar, and pulled it wide. I heard a gasp, and then she stepped back, gesturing for the visitor to enter. I saw Ellen peeping.

It was the gipsy girl from the shore, and an older woman.

They stood just inside the door, self-contained, waiting to see how they would be received.

It was my gran who spoke first – and perhaps assured their welcome. "Tinks inside my house! I never thought to see the day! ? Awa' out o' here, in God's name, an' stan' at the step where ye should be! Hae ye no' made trouble enough?"

Mam's lips tightened in annoyance.

The older woman answered gran. "We wish speech with Jean Main and her father. If it is not permitted, we will go." I'd never heard anyone speak like that – slow, formal, bell-like. I hoped dad would let me speak to them.

But it was my mother who replied. "This is my house," with a sharp glance at gran – "and all who come to it in peace are welcome." Here was mam speaking the same way! Gran's jaw dropped.

They put back their plaids from their dark, handsome faces. Neither had a decent cap, or a kerchief round her shoulders. The older one had brass hoops in her ears; I wondered for a moment if they could be gold, but only the Provost's wife had gold jewellery that I knew of; they couldn't be. Could they? She was tall, even taller than mam, who was taller by four inches than dad and most of the fisher folk. Her face was thin, with a large hooked nose; she certainly wasn't beautiful, but striking, and strangely elegant in her tattered red dress and green plaid, her black hair drawn tightly back and coiled round her head. The girl had cleaned her face and combed her dark ringlets; Donnie couldn't take his eyes off her vividness.

"My name is Margaret Davidson. This my daughter is also Margaret Davidson. We owe you and yours a great debt. Men would have been killed this day, and I have sons in the camp."

My mam stood, straight as a spear behind dad's chair, her head proudly high, her hand resting on his shoulder. "This is John Main, who fought Duggie Ralph. And there is our daughter Jean. We thank you for your kind thoughts, but Jean and my man did only what they thought was right. Men would have been killed here too. No gratitude is owed."

Margaret Davidson inclined her head gravely. "Maybe not," she said, "But we feel it still. The debt will be paid."

I remembered something. "These are yours, are they no'?" I held out the silver earrings to the girl. She made a move towards them, her face brightening, but her mother gestured and she stopped dead.

"Mistress Jean, I would ask you to accept them as a gift, a token of what else we may do for you."

The girl's face went quite blank, and I knew she was hiding a burst of temper – I did it myself. I was sorry for her, losing her earrings – but to have them for my own! But my mam's hand smoothly plucked them from me.

"Thank you. She is too young to wear them yet, but we will keep them for her when she is older."

The gipsy wife bowed again. "For you, John Main, I brought this." From a fold in her plaid she brought out a leather bottle, and I wondered if it was whisky; it was, but not for drinking. "This is the first run of the still, with good herbs infused in it. I can rub it in your arms and back and ease you."

Gran, muttering on the stool in the corner, struggled to her feet in alarm. "Ye'll put none o' your heathen devilish brews near my son! Lord God of Hosts, preserve us from all witchcraft, save us from evil, turn our souls from the offerings o' the Devil!"
"Ach, awa', Gran," said Donnie. "It's but a liniment. Like for the garron."

The gipsy's eyebrows twitched, but she did not smile. "Do you not need it, John Main?" she asked calmly.

Dad stirred, and spoke up for the first time. "Aye do I. An' I'd tak' help from Satan himsel' an' a' his imps this night. What do you say, Morag?"

For answer, she started to loosen the blanket from round him.

25

The gipsy wife made dad lie on his back in front of the fire, and peeled the blankets right down to his hips. The girl sat down by the hearth, and Donnie moved to keep sight of her. Then he just sat and watched, like me.

Gran grumbled off to her bed, catching Ellen peeping, and scolding her back under the blanket and clear o' such cantrips. We could hear her mumbling prayers as she climbed past Ellen and in with the twins, who slept in her bed. They didn't stir.

The gipsy slipped her plaid right off, rolled up the sleeves of the red dress, and knelt down. She poured some cloudy liquid out of the bottle onto her hands, and started to rub dad's chest and arms. At first he winced and grunted as the whisky stung his cuts, but after a while he relaxed and lay like the dead, while her strong, dirty fingers kneaded away, and I could see the skin moving more easily as she worked. After half an hour, she made him turn on his front, and rubbed his shoulders and back.

She hummed a tune as she swayed back and fore, rubbing rhythmically; it was the only sound in the house. Gran and the bairns were asleep. Donnie was dozing, his head fallen back against the wall. Mam was nodding on her stool.. Even the beasts were still. The red glow from the fire gleamed on dad's back, the red dress, and on the angles and few curves of the gipsy's face, and the scent of the herbs mingled with the tang of the whisky and the peat smoke. She rubbed and rubbed, slower and slower.

The girl stiffened where she sat by the fire, as if she heard a shout.

"Jean Main," the gipsy wife said, her voice quiet but intense. "Jean Main.

"Answer her," said her daughter. "You must answer. The Sight is on her. Listen to what she says, and mind on it. It's the truth. Answer."

"Jean Main!" the strange voice said again.

"I'm here," I replied. I should have felt frightened, but I did not. Nothing else stirred.

She turned towards me, her searching eyes dark and blind. "We're no' done wi' each other yet, Jean Main," she said. "We'll meet again, in the shadow o' the gibbet. Four times ye will bring life, Jean Main, or death. Ye're more important than ye ken. Ye will make a king, and break a king, but will ye ride the kelpie? Aye, we will meet. Four times. Seek out the kelpie, Jean Main."

It sounded a lot of nonsense. But the girl seemed to believe it, and looked at me in surprise, as her mother gasped, and shook her head violently. With her daughter's help, as if she was very weary, she rose to her feet, and moved to the door, her eyes fixed on me.

Dad sighed and yawned. Mam woke with a start. "Thank you for your help, Mistress Davidson," she said, blinking.

The gipsy turned her gaze on her. "Mistress? It's long since I was called that. Fine courtesy, Mistress Main, makes a fine house, and you have it. God bless you all." She gave me another long look and a nod, and left without a word more.

"Would you look at Donald there?" said mam, yawning. She poked him awake. "Come on, the both of you, gie me a han' tae get John tae bed. He's sound. I never thought he'd sleep this night. It's like magic – but dinna you say that to your gran, mind."

I promised, and helped persuade and lift dad into the big box bed without really waking him. As mam climbed in beside him, and shut over the doors, Donnie rolled in his plaid on his mattress in the corner and I went round the partition to my own bed. I slipped in beside Ellen, who was on my side as usual – when I shoved her over it was fine and warm.

For some reason, as I went to sleep I scarcely thought about the gipsy's prophecy. Riding a kelpie, indeed! And gibbets! And kings! What havers!

Little did I know.

THE CROFT

Catches the next week were good. Dad said the fish had been stirred up by the storms. The fishers, of course, said it was because I has been banned from the boats.

Dad rowed delicately, because of his jaw. Duggie rowed delicately because he had three fingers and four ribs cracked, and was strapped up like a new baby. They said little to each other, but got on with the work. Nobody commented on the fight at all.

I spent my time as usual, fetching in peats with the garron, but when the boats came in on the tide, it was Ellen, complaining bitterly, who took Dancer down to help haul them in. Then all the women gathered to carry home the fish when they were divided; two shares for the boat – dad got that; one for the nets – they were Jaikie's; one share for each man, dad, Donnie, Jaikie and Duggie; and a share divided, with a squabbling like gulls at a dead seal, among the old, the widows and orphans. That creel was always full, with the small and broken fish – for they were for eating, not selling – even if the others were scanty. Dad insisted; "Cast your bread upon the waters while ye have it, for it could be our turn next," he said, and Duggie scowled but said nothing, for he knew dad was right.

That meant we had four shares to deal with. When the creels were brought up, Gran, Ellen and I cleaned the fish. Mam, brought up on a croft, was too slow, but she sorted them out. Some for Gran to take up the street to sell at the Cross – as little as the Baillies would let us get away with. By law, fish should be on sale in the town each day, to draw in the country folk for the other traders. But prices were low there, only a penny for a dozen large herring, so we put up as few as we could. Then some for eating, salting, drying, smoking, pickling – mam was famous for her pickled fish – and on the right days, most for sale up the country.

Not many fisherfolk gutted their fish before selling them, but mam was always one for trying something different. She didn't see any sense in carrying fish trock away up the hills – and besides, the fish kept fresher. She made preserves with the livers and boiled the roes, and threw the rest to our own pig; and instead of maybe earning another farthing gutting them for the farmer's wife, she could carry more, and better, and earn extra money that way. It seemed sensible to me, but Nairn folk – especially the fishers – are thrawn, and slow to take up a new thing, especially if a foreigner tries it.

Every Tuesday and Friday, if there was enough fish for it to be worthwhile, my mother would carefully pack the creels for the country. Tuesday was the short trip, just a nine-mile round. Fridays, we went right up to Granda Mackay's croft, and stayed there overnight. It was near ten miles each way across the rough moor, and the twelve-mile round at the end of it. Too long to be done in one day.

The baskets for the pony held the plain fish, fresh, dried or smoked, all wrapped in clean bracken – haddock or herring, coley or ling, cod, flounders, dabs, sprats, and the mackerel that no fisher would eat, for it ate dead men. I had a small creel of my own, with fancies – cockles, prawns, boiled roes, horn jars of cod liver paste; and anything that the country folk had asked mam to bring up from the town, like nails or ribbons or salt. I got a plack – a quarter of a penny – for the carrying, sometimes. And mam carried the big blue and white jar of pickled fish in a special cradle

29

on her back. She would trust it to no-one else. Dad had brought it her all the way from Zeeland.

So the next Friday, ten days before the Michaelmas Fair, we wrapped our plaids well round us against the chill before the dawning, and shawled the baby warm. We led Dancer out of the house, and when he'd finished the capers that had given him his name, and could be trusted, we loaded the big square pony creels on his saddle, strapped Morag's carrying basket firmly in the middle, helped each other hoist up our own loads to our backs, picked up our knitting and went out to join Annie Ralph and the other women starting their rounds. Gran and Ellen would rise at the Taptow drum to see to the men and the wee ones, and get John off to school.

We walked up past the stalls being put up for the Friday market – I usually missed it – over the bridge and away up the path out of the town past Househill. It was nippy, and our breath puffed like smoke. At first it was quiet, but as they warmed up, the women started daffing and gossiping. What the Provost's wife had paid for her new red satin petticoats – Mary Main was out too late at nights – what the minister said to Elsa Mackenzie when she begged for some money to buy tea – was it no' scandalous, two pound a pound, even smuggled, Scots pounds, of course, no' sterlin' – Jimmie Bullock's hands were getting too twisted to work the nets now – last night Duggie Ralph – Sh! Annie'll hear ye. There were no secrets in Nairn; but they would not hurt the feelings of one of their own – and Annie's bruises from last week were barely starting to fade.

But they would not talk to me. From embarrassment, or whatever, they did not look at me or acknowledge me by more than a nod. Mam was coldly furious.

We were about three miles out of Nairn, just about at the turn-off to Raitloan, when we all turned to a shout and a rattling of hooves behind us. A gipsy lad was belting his bareback garron up the rocky path, waving to us to stop.

The women drew together for safety as he raced up, and slid down by my mother.

"Mistress Main!" he panted. "Ma sent me. There's reivers on the road. Ye've to take cover till they're bye."

"This close fae the toon?" cried Teena Fisher. "Never!" Everyone hesitated, but I saw from his face it was true.

"We canna chance it!" mam said, grabbed Dancer's reins and raced for the shelter of a scatter of birches up the hillside, Morag bouncing on the pony's back as we drove him up across the heather. All the wives gathered up their skirts and followed. The gipsy came more slowly, checking that no sign was left of our passage. We all struggled gasping through the brambles, past the first of the trees, and slowed down to look back. The lad urged us further in, right out of sight from the path. Then we put down our creels, so that we could run faster if we had to, and sneaked back to see.

I lay down in the moss beside the boy. "Was that no' you at the shore last week?" I asked.

He glanced at me, and returned his sly black eyes to the glen. "Aye," he said shortly.

"How's the quean?"

"Mag? She's fine. She's no' that pleased about lossin' her earrings, but it's her ain fault. She should just have kissed him an' been done wi' it, nae nonsense. Can ye no' keep that beast quiet?"

Dancer, excited by the sudden rush, was tossing and sidling, and might whinny and betray us. "I'm no' sure," I said. The gipsy looked disgusted, and went to its head. His own hairy pony stood panting but quiet.

Mam had lifted Morag down, and was feeding her to stop her crying. Dancer settled like magic, and we all watched in suspense.

Just as Teena Fisher was starting to mutter, "It's havers. He's leein'," a group of about a dozen Highlanders, in their huge plaids and bare legs, ran up the path from Foynesfield way. Two had muskets. Some of them had bundles on their backs, of goods they had stolen. They were driving four cows before them, udders flapping.

"Look at that!" whispered Annie Ralph. "That's thon red cow o' John Mackenzie's. A coorse bitch, thon. They'll hae trouble getting her hame wi' them – but she'll no' chase me doon the park again."

"Damn that Hielands!" muttered Jessie Main. "What call hae they tae tak' other folks' gear?"

"Some o' them's starvin' o' hunger," said mam. "It's been a bad year – an' it'll get worse."

"The sooner they a' starve theirsel's aff the better for decent folks, then," said Jessie, unabashed.

"Quiet!" the gipsy hissed. The men below us had stopped. One was looking all round, sniffing. "Damn that stinkin' fish!" the lad whispered. "Ye can smell it the far side Forres!" They searched the hillside with their eyes, and we lay tense, ready to take to our heels if they started our way, but at last one spoke, pointing back the way they had come, and they trotted on up the path.

"Thank you, son," said Betsy. The rest muttered agreement. She hesitated, and then offered him a halfpenny. He looked at it with contempt.

"Are ye sure ye can spare it?" he asked sarcastically. "If that's a' ye're worth, ye'd better keep it. Ye'll hae more need on it than me. It wisna ye I come for onyway. Ma telt me to tell Mistress Main. Thank her." He swivelled himself up onto his pony's back, nodded to mam, and cantered off, his bare feet brushing the heather.

The women looked at each other, and at mam. She gave them no help. At last, Betsy spoke for the rest. "Aye. Thank ye, Morag."

"Dinna thank me," said mam firmly. "If it hadna been for Jeannie last week, we'd ha' had nae warnin' the day. Thank her."

Again they looked at each other, and seemed to come to some unspoken agreement. They came up together, all six of them, and thanked me in turn. I blushed scarlet.

"Well," said Betsy, "I'm for hame. I'm no' goin' up the road after that lot, that's for sure, an' there's men enough at Rait to see to their troubles. There'll be nae fish selt the day. No' by me." The rest agreed.

"I'm for on," said mam. "The reivers are goin' faster nor us. We'll no' see them again. I'll risk it. Come on, Jeannie."

As we tramped along, I glimpsed the gipsy loon away up the hill above us, keeping watch. "Aye," said mam. "They say tinks aye keeps their promises, good or ill. I'm thinkin' ye've made a good friend there, Jeannie. I've never had a guardian angel afore!"

It took us another two hours to reach Granda Mackay's croft, but at last we turned the corner of the brae and there it was, a tiny patch of fields by the burn, hidden by the hills and a handy screen of pines from anyone not looking for it. As usual, there was a horde of my cousins screaming outside the little house. The cow had got up on the turf roof. The goats were at it every day, but the cow was heavier, and could break through the chimney hole. I ran down to help, and a shower of stones at last drove her down from her perch, and off up the pasture to be tethered where she could do no harm.

The children welcomed us, laughing, jumping and screeching round us. Granda Mackay and mam's oldest brother Gavin strolled up from the burn and greeted us warmly. Gavin's wife, Sheila, and the girls were out bringing in the last of the peats, but mam could aye make a cup of brose, they offered. They wanted some themselves, but like any highlandman, wouldn't venture on a woman's work. But mam wouldn't stay. She would leave the baby, but we were behind already, and we still had half the round to do that day. So it wasn't till we'd been to Coulmony House that was a good regular sale, and the steadings round it, and all the others down that end the glen, that we could go back to the croft for a rest.

I always loved the moment when you dived in through the thickness of the earth walls, like a rabbit going down its burrow, into the smoky dark and clutter of the one tiny room. Everything happened in that room. There was no partition, as we had at home, to cut off a sleeping place behind the fire. There wasn't even a chimney like ours, with its big hanging mantle where we smoked the fish. There was just a low wall built half across the floor, with the fireplace stones standing against it. The smoke rose gently towards a hole above, in the roof; but it usually stopped half-way, in a misty, eye-stinging layer about three feet off the earth floor. When you sat down, you were below it. Everything in the house, from the rushes that kept your feet dry off the mud on wet days to the rush matting that stopped bits of the turf roof falling in your soup, was either black with soot or grey with ash.

Behind the dividing wall, the cow and goats were kept in winter. In our house, there was a separate door for the animals, but not here. They'd soon have to be brought in. The byre end was half-full of hay, cut for feed through the long, dark months ahead. That was where mam and I slept when we visited.

It was cosy.

It was a dry night, so we left the creels outside, hung on a branch of the big rowan tree planted right by the door to keep away witches. No fox or polecat would try for them there.

Sheila and the girls were home from the peat cutting with a load each for the stack, and had made the dinner. We all settled gratefully to a big pot of pease porridge, with some mutton scraps in it, set in the middle of the floor. As we dipped our horn spoons, the talk started. Mam told about the fight, and the ban on me – they were disgusted – and then about the gipsy's warning of the reivers.

"You have a rare courage, Morag, to be coming on here after a scare like that," said Sheila. "Were you not scared, my dear?"

"I was not, then, Auntie Sheila," I said. I had the Gaelic as well as the English, of course. As all the wee ones looked admiring, I added, "I was terrified." There was a comfortable laugh all round the room.

We sat back, finished with the stew, licked our spoons clean and put them back in our pockets, and Sheila brought out a comb of new honey and a wooden platter of oatcakes.

Wee Shiona, the second youngest, piped up, "Tell us a story, Granda!"

"Ach, you and your stories!" the old man complained. "You're aye at me. I never get a minute's peace in this house to sit and think to myself. Besides, you've heard all my stories. I'll tell you no more."

We'd all heard this before. My granda was the finest storyteller in the whole glen, and at ceilidhs he was aye asked. "Aye, Father," said mam, "you've heard our news. My throat's sore telling it. Now it's your turn."

"Well, well," he said assenting. "What one will it be? Jeannie, you choose. Have you heard how Calum Beg stole the laird's own cow?"

But I knew that one, and after our close shave with the reivers, didn't feel like hearing how Calum, a great favourite with Rose of Kilravock, visited the laird one day. That night, as he was supposed to be sleeping in the laird's manager's own bed, he slipped quietly out and drove home a fat young heifer from the laird's herd that had taken his fancy the day before, and then as quietly slipped back. When the theft was discovered next day, the finger was pointed at Calum, but the grieve insisted that he must be innocent; hadn't he slept beside him all the night?

I remembered something the gipsy wife had said. "Tell us about kelpies, Granda," I asked. "Has anyone ever ridden one?"

"Ridden a kelpie?" Granda was surprised. "Aye, of course." I was taken aback – that wasn't what I had understood. "But none has ever come back to tell about it." Oh, dear.

"You know what a kelpie is, eh?" As little Shiona shook her head, Granda took her on his knee in his big chair by

35

the hearth, and his white beard tickled over her head as he spoke. Sheila quietly cleared away the pot, scraped out the last dregs for the dogs, wiped it and filled it with water for the morning's porridge. We all sat back on our creepie stools, happily full, to enjoy the story.

Granda's thin old voice deepened as he settled into his tale. "A kelpie is the fiercest, most dangerous spirit in all of Scotland, from Dunnet Head to Kintyre – aye, and maybe in England too, even. If you are late home some dark night, coming in from the market, or the alehouse, eh, Gavin? If you should ever be seeing a great black horse, or a fine black bull, quietly grazing by the path, turn yourself away! Never ever think it's a stray, and you can take it home. Never ever put a halter on its neck, however quiet it stands, however friendly it is. Even if the horse is saddled and bridled in silver, ready for you, never, never mount it.

"For if you set leg astride it, you're dead! You can never dismount, nor turn it, nor stop it, nor throw yourself from its back. For it is the Kelpie, and it will carry you off to the loch where it lives, and dive in, and you will never be seen again.

"Five year ago, Duncan Macalistair from Dulsie, just over the brae, and his son Tammas were walking home from the Geddes fair. Dark it was, and stormy, and the wind howling to rouse the dead from their graves. They were going through the wood at Belivat, just over the hill there, when Tammas stopped.

"'Look there!' says he to his father. 'Is that not the finest bull you've ever set eyes on? I wonder whose it is.' 'Never you mind,' says Duncan, wise man. But Tammas would not be told. 'It's lost,' says he. 'See how quiet a beast it is. It hasna even a nose-ring. I'll just take it home. When the Good Lord puts a gift like that your way, it would be a mortal sin to refuse it,' he says. Duncan warned him, but the stout lad would not listen. 'Kelpies?' says he. 'Ach, thats's just old wives' tales.' He put his belt for a halter on it, and its red eye rolled wild at him, so that he was frightened for an instant; but it followed his pull like a lamb its mother. 'See!' says he, pleased to be right. 'There's no danger at all it is!'

"But then the thunder rolled, and the light flashed, and did his father not miss his step and twist his ankle on a root? 'Here, father,' says Tammas, 'I cannot be carrying you all the way home. Climb you on the bull's back, and he'll carry you. See, I'll hold his head, that he'll not run off with you.' And his father, poor Duncan, half demented with the pain in his foot and the drink in his head, agreed. He got up on a fallen tree, and Tammas walked the bull before him. Easy, easy it came, as if it understood what was wanted of it, and it stood like a rock while the old man clambered on its back and grinned down at his son. And Tammas grinned back.

"Then, like lightning itself, the beast reared up, roaring its triumph like the thunder, and raced through the trees and away up the hill. Tammas, you may be sure, shouted and chased it, but how could he hope to catch it? He reached the top of the hill just in time to see the great kelpie, with his own father screaming and waving on its back, plunge into the Loch of Belivat, and the waters closed over the two of them with a great swirl, and there was nothing left.

"Tammas caused his own father's death, and he knows it. Since that day, he's a broken man."

There was a silence of appreciation, as we all sat in the warm, comforting firelight, thinking of Tammas, frozen with horror.

"So nobody has ever ridden a kelpie and lived, Granda?" asked Iain, my big fourteen-year-old cousin.

"No-one. They say that if you could ride a kelpie, and make it obey you, it would grant you your heart's desire. But who is horseman enough, or daft enough, to be trying it, and maybe failing?"

"Maybe I will some day. That would be a great thing, eh, mother?" said Iain.

Sheila looked at him with dismay. "Ach, no, son," she cried.

"Ach, mother!" he teased her. "Even I'm not that stupid." He looked at mam. "That's my news. I'm going to Glenferness House at Michaelmas. I'll be fourth horseman. Mr Mackintosh, the grieve – he says I've a real way with horses, and he'll give me a trial."

"Aye," said his father proudly. "It's himself will be first horseman to Lord Leven before he's done."

There was much talk about this prospect, and I forgot all about kelpies. But that night I had a thought.

In the morning, as we set out for our second round, I said to mam, "Mam, why dae I no' go intae service? If Iain can be first horseman to a lord, sure I can be a lady's maid, or somethin'."

She looked at me thoughtfully. "It's an idea. Ye dinna fancy workin' at the linen wi' your uncle James? Na', I can see that. Well. I was maid mysel' to Mistress Janet Rose o' Broadley, before I married. She's wed now, on Patrick Clark the surgeon. Aye, an' he's no' long made Depute Sheriff. She'll be lookin' for more help in the house. We'll see. We'll hae to dae somethin' about your hands – they're ower rough for a maid. But we'll see. She'll remember me kindly, I think. We'll see."

And so I took my next step to the shadow of the gibbet.

THE CLARKS' HOUSE

Mam was never one to dawdle. That same night she spoke with dad and the next day, though it was the Sabbath, was no day of rest. Every moment we weren't at the Kirk our needles were flying, making a length of blue wool from mam's basket into a new skirt and bodice for me, for mam said that my clothes looked like a midden – which did not please Ellen, who inherited them. Gran girned about not keeping the Sabbath, and was put briskly to hemming a new shift.

That night, when the bairns were bedded, Johnnie and the men were sent out a walk, and mam washed me all over, even my hair; the first time ever. While Ellen giggled and Gran gloomed I'd catch my death of cold, she scrubbed me with a rough towel and some of her precious soap, and I knelt shivering in my shift in front of the fire and wondered if it was worth it.

Next morn we set off for the High Street together, as soon as the men were away. My new clothes were fair grand; Jessie Ralph screeched, "Hey, hey, Queenie Jeannie!" and all my friends rushed to stare and jeer. I was thrilled. Mind you, I was feeling very odd. I'd hardly slept, with nervousness and cleanness. My stomach felt queerly empty, but I couldn't eat my porridge. And besides, mam had plaited my hair back so tight I couldn't move my eyebrows.

When we reached Mistress Clark's house in Kirk Vennel,

just off the High Street opposite the Tollbooth, the old prison, mam checked over me and herself to see were we as neat as possible. She was as nervous as I was. It was a fine house, with two rooms upstairs and two down, and a heavy oak door that swung open almost as mam knocked, startling her.

Mistress Clark was working in the kitchen, floury to the elbow. She was tiny, an inch shorter than myself, and her own children mostly towered over her so that she had a way of tilting her head to look up at them like a robin; but there was no doubt who held the reins in that house.

She dusted off her hands. "Of course I mind on you, Morag – Mistress Main, I should say. Are your husband and family well? A sup of tea? Celia, please. "She had scarce time to unlock the tea-caddy and measure out the expensive leaves before the kettle was ready. "Good lass. Now, what can I do for you?" She sat down with mam by the big table in the middle of the kitchen, and got straight into the matter.

She spoke in a gentrified voice. No wonder; she was gentry. The Provosts of Nairn had been Roses, father and son, for two hundred years.

I was too taken up with the wonders of the kitchen to heed the first part of the talk. There was a floor of smooth stones, not like ours of dried blood and burnt shell. And oiled linen in the window behind the shutters. And huge copper pots and pans, more than I could imagine a use for. That dough on the table – could it be wheaten flour? It didn't look like the rye that we used. And shelves and cupboards all round. And a great barrel in the corner with a tap in it – who drank all that ale?

I realised I was being spoken to.

"So you want a place here, Jeannie, eh? Turn round and let me see you, lass. M'hm." I felt like a sheep at the market. " Show me your hands." I had steeped them in milk for two hours to smoothe out the redness and chaps, but I needn't have bothered. "Aye, working hands, what I like

40

to see on a lass. We can teach you anything, if you're willing to work; and if she's your daughter, Morag, she'll learn quick." Mam looked cautiously pleased. "And we'll soon scrub the fish smell off her." Mam's face was interesting – after the scouring she'd given me the night before!

"Aye, well. True for you, Morag, I'm fair run off my feet these days. I'll give your lass a try. She'll sleep with Mary there –" the old woman skimming milk grinned gap-toothed at me – "in the kitchen corner, fine and warm, and have four hours off every two weeks to visit home. Has she shoes? No? She'll need them, for the kirk. Her keep, thirteen shillings and fourpence a year, and two pair of shoes."

"Sterling?" mam asked. A Scots pound was only worth a sixth of an English one, and some folk tried to cheat. Mistress Clark looked slightly offended.

"Of course."

"Her full keep? Firin'? Medicines if she's sick? No' that it's likely," she added hurriedly, "she's aye in health. Salmon how often a week?"

"No more than twice," said Mistress Clark, rather proudly. It was a poor man's meat.

"That will be quite acceptable then, Mistress," said mam formally; and that was it agreed.

"How soon can she start, Morag? I could be doin' fine with her right away," said Mistress Clark, "an' no' wait till the Fair. I've visitors the night. I'd be much obliged."

"No problem, Mistress Clark, she can stay here wi' ye now, an' I'll bring up her box this afternoon," said mam. "It's nae trouble."

And so quickly it was settled. Mam gave me a hug, bade me again be a good, biddable quean, and the door shut behind her on my old life. I hadn't said a word since we came in.

The first days I didn't know whether I was coming or going, what with not knowing where things were or how things should be done, but Mistress Clark was clear in her instructions and fair in her judgement, and with a bit of help from the others I got by without making too big a fool of myself. The worst was once when I was gawping at the spits – they were turned by a wee dog running in a wheel, a thing I'd never heard of. I knocked a china bowl of blaeberries, ready for a pie, right off the table with my elbow, and it broke. I thought sure Mistress Clark would send me straight back home in disgrace. But no, she gave me the choice – a birching or pay for it – so that wasn't too bad. I'd had worse from dad many a time. And I watched what I was at after that.

Everyone in the house worked hard, from the mistress herself down to me. There were two daughters, Amanda, who was fourteen, the eldest of the children, and Celia, ages with me. Miss Amanda was tall and fair, and a genius with pastry. None of her pies ever was tough, or soggy, or collapsed in the oven. She was nettle-tongued, and told me sharply to keep away from her pies until, as she said, the stink had worn off. Her mother frowned at her, and she flushed for her unkindness. She never really liked me.

But I agreed fine with the younger one, Miss Celia. She was short like her mother, but fair like her father and sister, and always bubbling with laughter and jokes. She couldn't cook to save a life, but her fine sewing was a real treat. She kept me right, the first day, pointing out where the cupboards were, and which bowls should be used for which mixes. She saved me putting cream for whipping in a bowl where onions had been pounded; if the smell had crossed from one to the other, and the cream ruined, I might well have been birched again, so I was grateful.

I had little ever to do with the boys, Colin and Patrick. They were away at school in Edinburgh most of the year, only home at holidays. We all had a craze one year for lifting peas from folks' gardens, till the master, as Depute Sheriff, had to pass a special bye-law forbidding it. He didn't know it was me and his own sons that were the worst culprits. But apart from that one summer, I saw little of them. They were aye at their own ploys.

There were two other kitchen servants beside myself.

Old Mary's teeth never met and her eyes never parted. It was gruesome to see her turn first one eye, then the other, on you, and you never knew whether she was watching or not. But she was kindly, and I soon found that though she was slow to start a job, once set to it she'd finish it even if the roof came in. I did the many wee jobs in the house, and the running-about ones, and she did the longer ones, and we worked well together. She snored, but no worse than my gran.

I didn't get on so well with the kitchen loon, Henny Grant. Mistress Clark kept a special birch rod just for him. The big barrel in the corner, that I had thought was for ale, turned out to be for water, and it was supposed to be Henny's job to keep it full, but he never did. I didn't mind – you got a fine gossip at the well, and an excuse for being late back. But whenever you shouted on Henny for a job, he'd be out in the stable with his brother Hugh, Master Clark's groom, dodging all the work in the house, and making up daft excuses with a huge, toothy grin. I had a lot of trouble with him playing tricks, till he found I would thump him if he bothered me too much.

Anyway, that first day, after the cooking was done and all the dishes had been scoured and racked, and all tidied for the morn – I worked so hard I scarcely saw the guests – I fell onto the mattress in the corner with scarce enough energy to pull the rug over me before I fell asleep. And I had to be up at the Tap-tow next day.

Within two days I knew I'd be happy with the Clarks. Mind, I wouldn't have if I'd been sulky or unwilling, for Mistress Clark had no patience with wilfulness or laziness, and her tongue could cut worse than her switch when she put her mind to it. She never let a fault pass unchecked, or good work unpraised. But when she saw that I tried, we got on fine.

On the Wednesday, I was sent out to buy fish for the dinner. I went to gran, of course, and got the best she had; Mistress Clark was no fool. On my way back I was gossiping with Katie Main when her eyes went past me and she froze up. It was the gipsy girl, Mag Davidson, behind me.

"What d'ye want wi' me?" I asked, my mind going first to the earrings safely stowed behind the loose stone in the fireplace at home.

"Ma's ta'en," she said quietly.

I didn't understand at first. "Taken? Taken where?"

"The Tolbooth!" she said impatiently. "She's for hangin'. She lifted a hen out o' Geordie Grant's henrun, an' she was spied. They gripped her yestre'en. She'll be up at the Assize the morn. Ye've to go see her."

"What? I canna walk off an' visit prisoners in the Tolbooth, just like that!" I said, alarmed. "Mistress Clark would have my backside raw!"

"I ken that," Mag shrugged. "But that's what she says. Ye'll find a way." And without another word she slipped away among the passers-by.

I went back to work, wondering what to do. Then, as if it was meant, a man came to the door looking for the surgeon, to come up the country to his son who'd cut his foot near off with a sickle. "Henny, go an' tell Hugh to saddle up," said Mistress Clark. "Jeannie, you go over an' tell the master he's needed. He's in the Tolbooth." My jaw dropped, and I stood hesitating for a second. "On you go, now!" she urged. "Dinna be shy. He'll no' eat you."

Wondering, I ran up and across to the old half-ruined Tolbooth. The master was there, talking to somebody in the one whole cell. When I gave him the message, he turned to shut over the door.

"Well, Maggie," he said, "I'll see ye in Court the morn."

"Aye will ye, Sheriff Clark," said a voice that was familiar, yet strange. "But ye'll no' be hangin' me. No' this time."

"I wouldna be so sure o' that, Maggie," he said, locking the door and handing the key to the jailer, who hung it on his belt. I couldn't get it there. "But I wish ye luck. Come, lass."

But as they went down the stair, I waited behind, and the jailer didn't see me. I tip-toed up. The barred peephole was too high for me to look in, but Margaret Davidson spoke to me without even seeing me.

"Jeannie Main. Mag found ye, then." The straw rustled as she came over to the door, and I saw her smiling down at me. " Ye've come quicker than I thought. I telt ye we'd deal together, did I no'?" Her voice was in the common speech, not clear and ringing like in my house. I didn't need to speak at all. "Ye'll save me, quean." Why should I? She answered the thought. " It's written. We're no' done wi' ane another yet." But how? "I dinna ken how. I just ken. Now off ye run, quean, or ye'll get into trouble, an' that wouldna help none. But mind, ye'll dae it. It's my life that's at stake." There was no tremor in her voice.

"Wha's that?" came the jailer's rough tones from below. "Ye're the Surgeon's servin' lass, are ye no'? Awa' hame wi' ye, ere I tell Mistress Clark on ye. She's a rare Tartar, yon ane. Aff wi' ye, quean."

"Thank ye, sir," I said politely, and scampered back before I did get into trouble, as they had warned me.

All that day, as I did my work, I puzzled how I could help the gipsy. Could I break her out, like a Mackenzie chief broke one of his sons out when the lad was arrested for reiving cattle? No, that wasn't practicable. What, then?

They were all talking about how she was a known thief, and this was the third or fourth time she'd been caught. She'd been imprisoned and put to stand three days in the jougs at Cawdor earlier in the year, and had been warned that the next time she'd be for the gibbet.

Mistress Clark was in a rare taking. "Heaven knows how your father'll do it, Amanda. You know he's as soft as summer butter. But it has to be done, and he'll just have to bring himsel' to it. We'll have a good meal for him the night, an' try to take his mind off it. Where's that recipe for stuffing I put in this drawer? And we'll stew some apricots as a treat – he aye likes apricot pie wi' almonds. Jeannie, put four eggs on to boil. Ach, this'll just ruin his stomach for days."

The evening reading of the Bible was longer than usual, and the prayers more fervent. Master Clark prayed for strength to do the Lord's work without flinching. We all knew he hoped for strength to do what he knew was his duty next day. He'd never conducted a capital case before, and dreaded the idea, being, as his wife said, a gentle man at heart. As a surgeon all his trade was to save life, not take it. By the time he'd reached the last Amen, our knees were all sore where we knelt in order, me and Henny in the back row in the parlour. That night, I could hear him tossing in bed, and rising to pray again, the thick boards squeaking under his weight, for he was a big man. I was praying my own self.

And that was what gave me the answer.

In the morning, I made sure to be the one to open the door for him as he went out to the Court. There was a great hammering and banging in the street, for today was the first of the three days of the great Michaelmas Fair and all the stalls were being set up. Master Clark, as Magistrate in the Assize Court that day, had little to do with organising the fair. He could perhaps have walked round the street with the other Bailies before the Court, but not this day. He was haggard and grey. Henny poked fun at him, saying that the master's mouth was tight as a duck's backside, all screwed up in his strangely flat face, but that was no fault of his, just an accident of birth. I felt heart sorry for him; such a kindly man should never have become a magistrate, whatever the honour – or the salary.

Like my dad, he was polite. Even in his own trouble of mind, he thanked me for opening the door, and that gave me the chance to say what I'd been rehearsing since four that morning.

"Please, sir, could ye answer me a problem? If ye've time?" I spoke as genteel and polite as possible.

He glanced down at me in surprise. Kitchen maids didn't generally address the master of the house without being asked. But I looked as innocent and worried as I could

– it was little acting I had to do – and he accepted the request as genuine.

"What is it, Jeannie?" He smiled kindly. "Aye, I've plenty time." He had indeed, it was still near two hours till the Court would sit.

"It's about the Bible, sir." That would hold him, I was certain.

"Aye? " He turned back into the house, and led me away from the stares of the others into the parlour. The mistress, fortunately, had gone up to a bedroom after putting his bonnet on straight for him. He took it off again now, scratching for the lice, and laid it on a chair. "Sit down, Jeannie. No, you'll no' get into bother." I perched nervously on the edge of one of the padded seats, hoping that there was no grease on my skirt to mark the cloth, or I'd get laldy. I was asking for enough trouble as it was, without cheekily sitting on the good chairs and maybe staining them.

"Now, what is't?"

"I'm not understandin', sir, about one o' the speeches o' the Saviour Himsel'. The minister read it out a month syne."

"I'm glad ye've been listenin' in the Kirk, an' no' just sittin' dreamin'."

"Aye, sir. I mean, no, sir," I said, virtuously, then hurried on before Mistress Clark should hear what was going on and interrupt. "It was about forgivin' your neighbour. Ane o' the Disciples asked how often ye must forgi'e a wrong, was it seven times, an' the Master said – "

"Seventy times seven. Matthew eighteen, twenty. No, twenty-two. I mind on it. Well, what do ye no' understan'?"

"I'm sorry, sir, but I dinna see how ye can sit in judgement on a sinner an' condemn him, when ye're telt to forgi'e him?"

He paused a moment, then smiled. My ear was cocked for the mistress coming, but all was still. He said slowly, "It's the differ between a sin an' a crime, Jeannie. I can forgive a sin, or even a crime against mysel', but wrong-doers have to be punished, for the protection o' the honest folk in the world. They have to be shown that wrong is wrong, an' if they'll no' take a tellin', they have just to be learned to turn to the right some other way. Does that answer you?"

"But if ye hang them, sir, how can they learn?"

He paused again. "That's a good question, Jeannie. The answer is that if ye hang one, it warns off the rest."

I took a deep breath. Last chance. "But that's no' what the Lord said, sir, is it?" I asked, as un-cheekily as I could. As he gave me a suspicious look, I tried my best to seem simply worried. Again, it wasn't hard.

"I must go," he said, rising.

"I'm sorry for keepin' ye, sir," I said. He hadn't answered me; it was the best sign I could have had that I'd given him something to think about. But would it be enough? It was all I could do, anyway. I offered him his bonnet with its fine gull-wing feathers.

As he put it on, askew as usual, Mistress Clark swept in. "I thought you were away, Patrick!" she said.

"Jeannie here had a question to ask me, Janet," he replied. "It couldna wait."

She gave me a searching stare. "Indeed?" she said briskly. "Well, she's a lot of work to do that canna wait either. Would you look at your bonnet – and I set it straight for you no' five minutes bye. Stand still till I sort it for you again. Jeannie, there's the floor an' the table to scrub before I can start the cooking."

I was out the door before she was finished, and on my knees with the heather stem scourer and the hot water before Master Clark was away out again. The mistress came into the kitchen and stood looking down at me for a moment. "The Master says ye're no' to get scolded for this," she said presently. Everyone else was listening hard, and Henny's ears were fair out on stalks. "But any more questions you've got, just you bring them to me. I'll speak to the Master if need be. Just mind on that. I'll no'

have a lass in my house that takes liberties. Now get on."
I'd expected a proper leathering – drat that gipsy! – but
if that was all the trouble I was going to get, I didn't care.
Henny looked disappointed, and maybe she realised it, for
she turned on them all, and him in especial, and sent them
scuttering to work.

All day, as I worked – and I was kept busy, with no
chance to get out to visit the Fair – I fretted about Margaret
Anderson. What had happened? Celia knew something
was bothering me, and stole me a piece of yesterday's
fruit tart from the pantry to hearten me; but it did little
good. However, when the mistress noticed the lack, she
blamed Henny, and as he'd deliberately spilled ashes
on my newly-cleaned floor to give me extra work, that did
cheer me. For a while.

Mistress Clark went, of course, to the Assize Court,
dressed in her brown second-best gown. She came back
with a face like thunder, and said nothing. I quaked. But
when at last the master returned, he was so relieved and
happy that it was clear all was well with him – and Margaret
Davidson. And if he was happy, I might still get away with
my impertinence.

Late on in the afternoon, when Mistress Clark and the
girls were out at the stalls, and the rest of us were taking it
easy for a minute, a friend of Mary's came by. She'd been
in at the Court, and could talk of little else.

"I dinna ken whit the toon's comin' tae. A fair disgrace,
so the man is. We'll hae a' the rogues in Scotland in the
toon by the New Year, noo they ken they can get awa' wi'
anythin', an' no' a thing done. Fair scandalous, so it was."

Her wet mouth dipped greedily to the ale-cup. "Takin'
the Word o' the Lord in vain, so it is. Matthew eighteen,
twenty-twa he said – forgi'e a man seeventy times seeven.
Whit trock! A' for a tinkie wife! Aye, she's tae be punished – if ye can ca' it that. She's tae be whipped through
the toon, an' her ear nailed tae the Tron gate an' cut aff, an'
branded on the cheek, an' then banished the toon on pain

o' death. Whit's that tae a tink? A guid hingin's whit she needed. That wad learn her, eh? We haena had a hingin' in the toon for far ower lang. Aye, a fine sicht, a hingin', so it is. It does a'body guid – except the corpse, heh, heh!" Her belly bulging under its greasy apron wobbled as she giggled. She was disgusting.

I went to the door to throw out some slops. Mag Davidson stood on the other side of the street. She said nothing, just looked at me and smiled, and the mistress saw her as she came in.

She called me to the parlour. "Why did you do it, Jeannie?" she asked firmly. It never occurred to me to lie, and I told her the whole story. I didn't know if she'd believe me, but she had Highland blood herself and knew about the Sight. When I'd finished, she considered a moment. Then she said, "I dinna know, Jeannie, if you grasp just what you did. Subvertin' the course o' justice is a very serious matter. You could be jailed for it. But this one time I'll overlook it. This once, mind! So no more gipsies, and no' a word to a soul. Ye understand?"

"Aye, mistress," I said. I understood fine. If word got out that the Depute Sheriff had done what his kitchenmaid suggested, I might be jailed, but he'd be the laughing stock of Nairn. Of Scotland, even.

She looked at me again. "Aye," she said, thoughtfully. She held out something to me. "Here. The morn, you an' Celia can go round the fair." It was a sixpence! "But stay awa' from tinks. They just mean trouble."

She was too late, though.

I didn't go to see Maggie Davidson being whipped. Henny was all disappointed – she hadn't screamed, even when they cut off her ear. He might as well have stayed at home, he complained.

THE FAIR

For the next two years I was very happy with the Clarks. Once the mistress realised that I wasn't going to fill her house with gipsies, and stopped watching me like a hawk for any more impertinence to her husband, we settled down fine. The work was harder than at home, mostly because of Mistress Clark's unnatural belief in cleanliness, but shared among all of us we could cope – and still find the time for a deal of fun.

Miss Amanda, five years older, had little to do with me except in the kitchen. That suited me well, for she was far too fine for my taste. But Miss Celia and I had a grand time. She was a flightery, happy lass, and a fine lot of scrapes she got me into.

I mind one day, the first summer I was there, Mistress Clark sent Celia and me out to gather wild rose flowers for her rose petal wine. She had a name for it in the town. We went away off up the river. By the time the baskets were full, we were far beyond where we were allowed to go, and in trouble anyway, so Celia suggested we take off our clothes and she'd teach me to swim like the boys did. I refused – no fisher ever could swim; why prolong drowning? But I wasn't a fisher any longer, she said, and it was so hot – and there was nobody about. In the end, we played about so much that our hair and all our clothes got soaked, past drying before we reached home.

We decided – Celia decided – that the only thing to do was to make the most of the situation. Before I knew what she was at, she pushed me right in, clothes and all, and jumped in beside me.

On the way home, we practised our story. I had fallen in – which was half true, at least – and Celia had bravely saved me from a dreadful death. At first, it was going to be me who saved Celia, but I thought the mistress would be pleased to have a daughter that was a heroine. We put a lot of work into the details, acting it out all the road home. It was a work of art.

The mistress listened to us without a word, her head to the side as usual. Then, still without a word, she stripped and birched us both equally, and set us to washing out our wet dresses. We thought it was most unfair of her. They weren't even our best clothes – and we'd brought back the roses.

A lot of changes took place in those two years. The Sheriff of Nairn died, and his successor appointed his own cousin as Depute Sheriff. Master Clark wasn't sorry to lose the post, but remained a Bailie. His skill as the town's surgeon was tested to the limit in March, 1745, in an epidemic of measles. Old Mary died of it, and about fifteen other people in Nairn.

My own family was badly hit; though none died, the twins, now eight, were very ill, and were slow, slow to recover their strength. Although their minds were so weak – the master said they had maybe been damaged at birth, and they would never grow up properly – they had always been happy, strong and healthy, and no trouble to keep clean and content. Now they were girning all day, not eating, and needing gran's love and care more than ever. She had little time for anything else. She took the measles herself, and grew deaf after. Mam had a hard time.

It was that August that Prince Charles Edward Stewart came to Scotland, to try to win back his grandfather's crown, that his father hadn't succeeded in regaining thirty years before. He landed away on the west coast somewhere, and many of the clans gathered to him. But it had little interest for me, though the master and mistress were excited and upset by the news; for me, my cousin Donald's wedding and building his new house were far more important.

I noticed, though, when General Cope marched his army through Nairn to deal with the rebels. I turned out to cheer with all the rest, as the grand men in their fine red and white uniforms and three-cornered hats marched by. It was the first time I'd ever seen an Englishman. They looked quite ordinary – I was a bit disappointed. They stayed overnight, and my Auntie Ellen was so excited by the Lobsters camping just across the river from her house that she had her latest child three weeks early. It was called John Cope Main, in honour of the General, and he visited her before he left, and gave the babe a whole golden guinea. That was a wild night in the Fisher town. I wasn't let go down – it wasn't safe, said the mistress. She was maybe right.

I learned a lot, those two years. How to look ahead and provide for the seasons to come; making soap, candles, wine, cordials, jellies; preserving and storing all kinds of food, flour, meat and meal, honey, fruit, vegetables, game – about fish I could teach the mistress; caring for linen and wool, hangings and blankets, fur and leather; sewing – though I was no hand at more than a plain hem, I learned to tell good work from bad; cooking that mam never dreamed of, with spices she couldn't afford, and delicacies brought in from far lands – raisins, sugar, dried figs and dates, even a lemon, once, that the mistress let none but herself lay a finger on; serving and behaving as was fitting in a fine house. For though the house was not large, the mistress remembered her father's home, and brought up her own family to be ready to take their place in the finest houses in the land. And she was generous with her instruction to anyone who wanted to learn.

I soaked in the new knowledge as a dry cloth sops up water. I forgot all about the gipsy, and that rubbish about gibbets and kelpies and kings, and concentrated on the arts of the housewife; but better even than that, on reading and writing. For Miss Celia, finding that I could do no more than print my name, took a fancy to teach me.

Miss Amanda and Miss Celia did not go to the parish school. It was a class of about seventy boys, ruled with a bundle of strong birch rods and a practised arm by the minister, Mr Alexander Rose Macnaughton, whom my brother Johnnie called Rosy Nosy for obvious reasons, when you saw him. That class was rough, often rude, and occasionally rowdy, when the fisher loons and the lads from up the town, who were of Highland stock, carried on the old feud.

Mistress Clark and some other mothers of young would-be-ladies arranged that the minister should hold a small, genteel class for them three evenings a week. They learned to read, write a clear hand, keep accounts, and speak some French; what was needed for a civilised household. And Miss Celia, out of some missionary whim, offered to pass it on to me.

After the midday meal was cleared, before the afternoon's work was properly started, Mistress Clark usually put her feet up for an hour. The servants, naturally, took an hour's rest too, unless she had given strict instructions that some task must be done. This was the hour when I could learn what I had so often longed for.

Mistress Clark was quite agreeable, but the minister was not. He came to complain one afternoon, but got short shrift from the mistress. When I took the tea-tray into the parlour, his long nose was fair glowing with emotion, and his dull little eyes had more life in them than usual. He sat silently fuming until I left.

"You must understand, cousin," – for he was a far-out cousin of the mistress, like all the Roses – "you are doing the girl no favour. What does a simple girl need with learning? She is not fitted for it. It will merely confuse her, make her unhappy with the position of life for which the Lord has intended her. She will get above herself."

"Aye, she does that frae time to time," Mistress Clark said drily, "but a dose o' castor oil soon sorts her." He snorted in disgust, and I could scarce help giggling, my ear pressed to the keyhole. He began to argue again, protest in his scratchy voice, between sups of tea and bites – big bites – of seedy cake, but after a while she cut him off. "As for her position in life, Cousin Alexander, that's a matter for her to decide on. She's bright an' she learns quick, an' the way she's goin' on this past while, she'll end up married on a member o' the Council some day – if she doesna over-reach hersel'. No, I'll not argue with you. You can come in an' lift the tray now, Jeannie."

I was in the door and half-way across the room before I realised her voice hadn't raised. How did she know? I sometimes thought Mistress Clark had a touch of the Sight herself.

So for two years I worked at the reading and writing, and it came easy to me. My dad wasn't too sure about me learning something he couldn't do, but I stuck at it. By the 45 Michaelmas Fair I could make a good stab at most of the Bible, though not the begats; the long names were beyond me yet. And I could write a reasonable letter.

That Fair I knew better what I was at, and could be a help to Mistress Clark at her buying. The first day, we got in all the main provisions for the winter; three different kinds of oatmeal, dried peas and beans, stockfish – dried salt cod and salmon – salt, wheat flour, salt meat, eggs to lard and store under water, apples, nuts, honey, vegetables; and the other necessities, linen, rope and twine, thread, hay, feathers for mattresses, woollen and linen cloth, leather, peeled rushes to dip in lard for lights, wax and wicks for candles, alum, bleach, bowls, brushes, and all the thousand things the household would need. My feet and legs were aching with running up and down to the attics and cellars, stowing all away safely, and my throat was sore with shouting on Henny and Hugh to help.

The Friday was the main Fair Day. All the stalls were

up, and the traders were in from all over, with the fancy goods, as well as the plain stuff, and the entertainers, the gipsy jugglers and fortune-tellers and the ale-wives. The next day would be for bargains, for those willing to risk leaving getting what they wanted the first days, hoping to get it cheap when the traders didn't want to have to carry it away again. There was little trouble; there were twenty good men picked to be watchmen to prevent any disturbance. That year my dad was one.

Mistress Rose had a goose for the dinner, and it was on the table, all prepared for the spit, fine and early. Then she set out, with Miss Amanda. Miss Celia, and myself, to tour the stalls, the crowds jostling round us. Henny was long gone, of course.

We stocked the medicine box with poppy, camphor, senna, and a dozen other things hard to come by, and paid an unbelievable amount of silver for cinnamon, ginger, pepper and cloves. Then we headed on down the street, slowly, gathering by the way. Ribbons, embroidery thread, two needles and a paper of pins; a set of yew-wood bowls that nested inside one another; ten pounds of sugar; a pewter jug; a new butter churn, to be delivered; a word with my mam as we passed her stall; a full roll of fine lawn for petticoats, to be sent, thank goodness; and then on down to the horse lines, by the Bridge.

Mistress Clark had decided that with all the upset, the Rebellion and the Highlanders wandering all over, she would feel safer with a watchdog. The wee spit dog, Dandy, was a snappy wee brute, but no real protection. Sure enough, at the horse lines, among the hairy Shelts and prettied-up old nags, she found a group of gipsies with a huge, snarling hound.

I was wary of it, and the young ladies stayed well clear, but nothing scared the mistress. "Whose is this dog? Is it for sale?" she asked the men, stepping up firmly.

One bulky young man eyed her with the sly, sideways half-smile of the tinker folk. "Anythin's for sale, at the right price, leddy," he said. Then to my astonishment he looked at me and gave a half-bow. "Good day, Mistress Jean," he said. The other men nodded gravely. I gaped. The mistress flushed with annoyance, but saw from my face that I was as surprised as herself .

"What price would you ask, then?" she said.

"Five shillin'," he replied promptly.

"What? It's no' a flock o' sheep I'm wantin'," she snapped, and the bargaining started. I couldn't but admire her. It took her just two minutes to beat him down to tenpence, and tell him to bring it up to the house.

"Your gipsy friends again, eh, Jeannie?" she questioned me as we left, but finally accepted that I'd never set eyes on him before to my knowledge. We collected more goods on the road up – a gingerbread for Celia, some sugared almonds for Amanda, two white hareskins to trim a hood, a length of lace, ten ells of a fine tan and green striped woollen cloth. My arms were growing longer by the minute.

The big gipsy was waiting for us at the door, his dog on a rope. "Ah, good," said the mistress. "Come in an' settle your brute by the door." She unlocked the door, swung it open, and stepped in. The gipsy followed us, his dog at his heels.

Suddenly, the man shouted and fell sideways, bumping me into the mistress. The hound leaped on the table, where the goose was lying, seized it in its enormous jaws, and bounded out over the top of me and away. The man scrambled to his feet, again getting in my way, and raced after it, shouting, "Dinna fret, mistress, I'll bring him back!"

Mistress Clark screamed, and ran after him. I dropped the basket, and followed, Celia after me. As we ran, half the folk in the town took up the chase, shouting through the stalls, following the dog and its owner round the streets, scattering the sheep and beasts in the cattle market, dodging in and out the Shambles. The mistress had a grand turn of speed, for a fine lady in six petticoats and her tight plaid jacket. We went round the town a second time, overturning piles of cabbages and baskets, frightening the horses by the smithy, twisting round corners and under carts, until at last we lost track of them in the gardens up behind the Horologe Stone.

It was the best hue and cry there'd been for years in the town, but the tink and his dog were just too slippy for us. At last we had to stop. There was no sign of them. The crowd – the ones that had lasted the pace – laughing and shouting, took the mistress' halfpence with nods of thanks and headed back for the ale stalls, and we turned home.

Mistress Rose, crimson with running and annoyance, glared at me. "Tinks!" she panted in disgust. "We'll never see him again! Or his dog. Or my fine goose! An' he's away wi' my money, too! You'd think I'd know better, at my age!. Ach, well. Jeannie, run down to your mother and get us a pot o' pickled herrin' for the dinner. I must have somethin' for the master, an' I'm past starting cooking now." As Celia, gasping, came up with us, she added, "Aye, an' you can go too. You need the exercise, it looks like. Where's Amanda?"

"I'm thinking she stayed in the house, mistress," I said.

"You know she canna run, mam, she says it's no' lady-like," said Celia.

"I'll ladylike her! It's those stays she laces so tight! But it's maybe as well somebody stayed in, or we'd have lost everything in the house by now. Aye. Well, off you go, Jeannie. Dinna be long, now. Ach, here's the Bailie's men, too late again! Where were you sleepin', eh? Or were you testin' the ale?"

Celia and I laughed ourselves silly as soon as we were out of Mistress Clark's sight. Every few steps a fresh detail of the chase would come to mind. The way the geese had scattered into John Stone's peas! The cow that had leaped half over the garden wall as the dog ran under its belly, and stuck like a see-saw! We had to stop and laugh again and again.

It took us long enough to reach mam's stall. She was just

packing up. She'd heard the noise of the chase, of course, and seen the tail-end. We spent some time telling her about it. But at last she turned to the big jar and started to pick out two dozen of her finest herrings for us.

Just then there was a shouting and commotion at the ale stall two up. "Ach, it's Duggie Ralph again!" mam said in disgust, craning her neck to see over the crowd. "He's aye drinkin' in Christian Sutherland's ale-shop these days. Annie never gets to keep a tenth o' what she gets for the fish. She has to keep some hidden to buy food, an' if he ever finds out, Lord help her!"

"It's a good thing he hasna any bairns, mam," I said.

"Maybe that's the trouble," she said reflectively. "Annie had a bairn by her first man, but they both died wi' the sweatin' sickness. An' then she wed Duggie, an' never had another. So it's no' her fault. Maybe if he'd had a bairn – but who's to ken? It might have made no differ at all. Miss Celia, will ye tak' the bowlie, now? Ye'd best be runnin', or it's a skelpin' ye'll get, an' no' your dinner."

"Aye, we'd best be off, Mistress Main, thank you," said Celia. She took the bowl of fish and turned – straight into Duggie.

He was reeling down the street, staggering and dirty, cursing and spitting at anything in his way. Naturally, all the folk stepped aside, but the walls and stalls didn't. He was in a vile temper, muttering oaths to himself and ready to lash out at any touch, and as Celia bumped him he snarled and raised his hand to her.

I jumped forward, without thinking, and grabbed his arm for a second. "Stop it, Duggie Ralph!" I shouted. My idea, as far as I had one, was more to keep him out of trouble than anything else. Celia, startled, began to curtsy and apologise, but he paid her no heed. His bloodshot, puffy eyes were fixed on me.

"My God!" he bellowed, his gap-toothed mouth gusting ale at me from in the stained yellow beard. "It's you again, ye red-headed bitch! Lay a han' on me, would ye? I'll learn ye manners, ye – " He started foul-mouthing me, and lurched towards me, fists swinging.

Mam stepped between us, shouting for the watch, but a swing of his arm pushed her back, and she slipped on some fish guts and fell. He came after me without pausing.

I wasn't too bothered. I'd seen drunk men in plenty before, and Duggie was so far gone a blind man with the gout could have dodged him. As long as I kept out of his grip, there was nothing he could do. But Celia didn't know that. More gently reared, and protected from wild violence and drunkenness, she was horrified, and certain this huge, drooling maniac was going to tear me apart.

With enormous courage she came to my rescue. Setting the bowl down carefully – the silly things you think of at such times! – she tackled him like a terrier going for a bull. Her fair hair flying from her slipping cap, she clutched at his right wrist and hung on grimly, shrieking as he swung round and lifted her off her feet, her blue skirts flying. I dived back in to help her, gripped his other arm, and for a few seconds the two of us were swirled round him like clothes on a washing line. As I flew through the air, I thought that this was the daftest thing I'd done in a long time. Mistress Clark would be furious – and quite right too. Then he shook me off, and before I could get back in there, he clouted Celia, just as he had done the gipsy girl two years before. She let go, stunned, and fell back into the stall, crashing into the post where mam had hung the big Zeeland jar of pickled fish. The strap slipped, and the jar fell thudding down on her head and broke.

There was a sudden hush. All the people watching, who had been laughing at the two girls and the huge man, gasped as they saw that real damage was done. Celia was lying unconscious, a great gash in the side of her head, the blood gushing down scarlet over the gleaming silver and cream fish, and the blues of her dress and the broken jar. It looked quite pretty.

Then mam knelt down beside her, gathering her protectively into her arms and cursing Duggie at the pitch of her voice. I picked myself up. Shouting and swearing, Duggie started for me again, and dad and two of the other watchmen finally pushed through the crowd and grabbed him.

There was a considerable struggle before they subdued him and got him away to the Tolbooth, but all the men, shocked by Celia's injury, helped, and at last he was dragged off. Somebody ran for Mistress Clark, and Celia was carried carefully home, a strip of mam's petticoat tied round her head. I picked up the bowl of herring, that had survived untouched all the flying feet round it, and followed, wondering what would happen.

Fortunately, Celia was not seriously hurt. She recovered her senses in an hour, and only had to keep her bed for two days. Her version of what had happened agreed with mine, but the mistress still looked black at me for a while. But what could I have done?

Duggie came up before the Assize next day. Assault was a serious matter, especially when it was on the daughter of one of the Bailies, and Depute Campbell took a severe view of it. Duggie was sentenced to ten dozen lashes, two dozen on each of the next five Saturdays. Mam's jar wasn't mentioned, though he could have been made to pay for it. Mam said she'd not put that trouble on Annie too.

I was called as a witness, of course, and as the sentence was spoken Duggie's eyes fixed on me with an unspoken threat and promise of vengeance. I couldn't stop shivering.

Three weeks later, while dad and Duggie were hauling in a net, the coble lurched. It was windy and choppy, and Donald and Jaikie were busy trying to hold the boat steady to the wind, and didn't see what happened. Somehow dad, who had been in and around boats all his life, lost his footing. He turned as he fell, and his back landed on one of the oar pins, sticking up from the side of the boat.

He was carried up to the house, paralysed from the waist down.

Nobody was so upset as Duggie.

THE BONE AND
THE WORD

When I visited home, I couldn't connect the sick, fevered hulk moaning and tossing on the pallet by the fire with my strong, healthy dad. I remembered the young ones, watching in horror after the big fight. My mind circled again and again, as it had done then. Was it my fault? Or would it have happened some time, as Donnie kept telling me, whatever I did? I didn't know what to think.

After a week, mam came up to the Clarks' to see the mistress. She was in a sore state.

"I'm sorry to see you in such trouble, Morag," Mistress Clark said, bringing her in to sit by the fire. "Anythin' I can do, you just have to ask."

"You're kind, Mistress Clark," mam replied. She hated ever asking for a favour, and I could see her shrinking inside. "There is somethin'." She paused to wrap her plaid tighter round her, as if she was cold even in the warmth of the hearth, and then took a deep breath. "I just canna manage wi'out a loan o' Jeannie." She gripped my hand tight, tight as I sat beside her.

Mistress Clark, naturally, looked surprised. "A loan?" she asked.

"Aye, a loan. I'll tell ye." Mam shivered.

"Do that," said the mistress, pouring her a glass of the claret wine she usually kept for favoured guests. Mam sipped it cautiously – she usually drank ale, of course – and it seemed to relax her, for she went on more easily.

"Ye ken whit's happened?"

"Aye, the master told me. Your man'll no' walk again, he says, barrin' the will o' God."

Mam smiled bitterly. "The will o' God's a strange thing, Mistress Clark. I had a fine, straight man last week, an' here I'm now wi' a cripple to be cleaned an' dressed like a bairn. As if I hadna enough bairns already. But it could be worse. Johnnie's had to gi'e up his hope o' bein' a lawyer an' leave the school to tak' his dad's oar, but he's just old enough for it. Donnie spoke up for him. When his dad, my good-brother Donald, was drowned, my John spoke for Donnie to be third oarman in the coble, though he was but ten, an' now Donnie's spoken for Johnnie. Duggie Ralph doesna like it, but Jaikie has agreed."

Poor Johnnie, I thought. He had hated the fishing, but now he had to leave the school to earn the money we needed – for as owners of the boat, we had to pay the size tax, and that was thirteen shillings and fourpence Scots each week. He'd be hauling and struggling at an oar all his life now – in the same boat as Duggie Ralph.

"There's no word how – ?" the mistress inquired.

"Na'. John says he doesna ken, an' Donnie an' Jaikie werena watchin'. But I ken, Mistress Clark. An' God kens." She took a deep breath. "Anyway, I need Jeannie a couple o' days a week. John's a heavy man, Mistress Clark, an' his mother canna manage him, even wi' Ellen's help, so I canna be awa' frae the house more nor a few hours. So I canna do the round to Coulmony. But if ye'd let Jeannie go off on Friday, an' back on Saturday – ye'd cut her wage, o' course -"

"That will be quite all right, Morag," said the mistress, firmly. "She'll go, an' no nonsense about less wage." And held mam's head as she wept for relief.

I started that same week. Taxes and buryings don't wait. With winter weather coming on, and only Johnnie instead of dad, the boat couldn't go out as far or in such choppy weather, and Duggie didn't know the fish like my dad, so the catches would be less anyway. But what we got had to be sold well.

We had some money hidden with my silver earrings behind a loose stone in the fireplace, of course, but that had to be hoarded for absolute necessity. It would be a hard winter.

Margaret Davidson had left the town after her punishment, but hadn't gone too far. Three weeks after dad's accident, she came to the door one night when I was visiting, risking her life if she'd been taken, to see was there anything she could do. Even gran was glad to see her. She examined dad's back in the dim light from the crusie lamp, and shook her head regretfully.

"No, Mistress Main," she murmured in her clear, formal voice. "It's in the hands o' the Lord." Gran sighed and nodded." All I can say is I've seen this mend afore now, but nobody knew why. Just for no reason, the knot in your man's back could untie itsel' sudden, an' he'll be able to move again. But you must help him prepare for that day. Leave him, an' his muscles will wither like dry leaves."

She showed mam how to rub and exercise dad's legs to keep them supple, and gave her a new ointment to prevent bedsores. Then, dad sighing with relief at being let lie still again, she went to the door. On the step, she turned to me. "We're no' done yet, Jean Main," she whispered. "Three times more, mind. Are ye mindin' on the kelpie?" And she vanished in the dark.

"What was that, Jeannie?" asked mam, but I couldn't tell her. It was far too daft.

Fortunately for us, the weather that winter wasn't very stormy, and the boat could go out. But the cold was fierce.

Dad, lying on his mattress by the fire, felt it rise from the earth below him, seep in through the three-foot-thick walls, and whistle in the draughts round the door. He suffered the pain of his back, and even his frustration at not

64

being able to move, with courage and surprising patience, when you thought how active he had been. But the cold, that he'd always been able to work off before, fairly tortured him.

The rest of us suffered, too. Every trip, I brought in Dancer loaded with wood from the hills, and we'd had a good peat-stack. But Johnnie was just crippled with cramps and aches. Mam rubbed him, as the gipsy had shown her how to rub dad, but he still moved like an old man. A lot of that was Duggie Ralph's fault.

Everything that went wrong – a net torn by seals, a lost line, even a spraying from a cross-wave – Duggie took out on Johnnie. As well as the usual raw sores off wet clothing, and bumps from the boat, the loon had bruises all over him from the kicks and blows he was given. And the constant narking speech was just as bad, swearing and cursing, trying every way to make Johnnie feel bad, talking about his useless crippled dad and his bitch of a mother – Johnnie told me about it sometimes, near crying with rage, where our parents couldn't hear. But what else could he do?

The other men would, or could, do nothing. Donnie had a new baby, and Jaikie was getting on. They'd not risk trouble standing against Duggie for a lad who was no worse treated than many. They'd done their duty by him, getting him into the boat at all, and that was that. Johnnie just had to bear it, and promise himself what he'd do when he was older and stronger.

I had not a bad winter myself. I had dreadful chilblains on my softened feet until dad suggested I get a pair of wooden clogs, such as he'd seen in Zeeland. The cobbler made them for me, and I could stuff them with wool and have protection against the ice. They were grand for sliding. Mam made me warm stockings, I wore the heaviest plaid, and at first I fair enjoyed my trips up to the croft.

There was little snow, even up in the hills. Nairn was always milder than most places, but that winter, though it was bitter cold, the sun shone bright and the sky was blue and high. I was young, healthy, well-fed – thanks to Mistress Clark's generous nature; there were a good few lasses in the town who were half-starved – and there were far worse things to do than tramp up through the crisp frost, with a warm pony handy to heat up my fingers when I couldn't knit well any longer under my plaid. There was so little snow that I'd be walking up the same track I'd made for week after week. The snow lay patchy, vanishing from the south slopes without ever melting, a strange thing.

One thing, there was no risk of the fish going bad.

All winter my family fed fairly well. Whenever the fishing was specially poor, something would appear as if left by the fairies on the doorstep – a rook, a pair of thrushes, half a hare, a couple of squirrels, a bittie venison, once a cut of stolen mutton; not much among seven, but it put them by. Ellen and Isaac fetched in cockles and seaweed as usual. Mistress Clark sometimes sent down a bite, too – the end of a pie, a baggie of meal, or the like. Dad, growing whiter and thinner every time I saw him, tried to joke about living like a laird, and mam, with new lines on her face, would carry on the joke – too long.

But the strain wore them all down. Mam was nursing dad and the sick twins; gran was growing old, shaky and deafer – though not dumb; Johnnie was half dying in the boat and coming in silent and grim – and dad saw the bruises, but could do nothing, and fretted; Isaac was needing breeched, and full of destruction; and Ellen was whining, and having to be driven to work. Only wee Morag was happy.

It was long till spring.

We had no time nor interest to attend to the world's news. Master Clark might worry about the Prince invading England, and near putting King George off his throne, or about the events we heard of – a battle at Prestonpans, where Sir John Cope was thrashed – Auntie Ellen was mortified, as if she had anything to do with it, and stopped calling, one of the few bright spots that winter – the taking of Carlisle, the Highlanders retreating from Derby, the battle of Falkirk; but my family and I were too weary to heed anything.

I was as weary as any of them. The round was long and the creel heavy, and before and after I had to toil extra hard to keep up with my work at the Clarks'. They couldn't take on another lass to help me, with the master not being Depute Sheriff now, and they were so good to me I had to do my best for them. Celia helped me as much as she could, but even so by March I was bone-tired.

Sometimes I thought about the kelpie. Granda Mackay had said if I could ride it, I'd get my dearest wish. I wished dad was well again. But where could I find a kelpie? And could I ride it if I did? And would I dare try?

Granda's story had told of a kelpie in Loch Belivat. So as I went to and from the croft, I formed the habit, tired as I was, of climbing up to look down on the black loch in its cup of blue-shadowed white hills. It was an eerie place, pleasant in summer, but dark and forbidding in the chills of winter. I never saw anything. What would I have done if I had?

I often met the gipsies while I was out. Mag Davidson and her brother Aelec would keep me company, and carry the big creel sometimes. They gave me advice on the gipsy ways; not to carry all my money together, but in separate pouches to try to save some if I was robbed; to hide some by the road if I would be coming back that way, for the same reason; how to set hidden snares on my way out, for rabbits or birds, and clear and lift them on the way in; what to do if I was attacked, or sprained an ankle and no-one by; and many other hints. I think they liked showing off to me. It was good fun learning to poach. They helped and cheered me a lot.

One day early in March, when I was on my first round to Coulmony, they both appeared in great excitement. "Ye've to wait on the day, an' dae the other round the morn," said Mag. "Ma says there's somethin' for ye tae see this nicht. We've to tak' ye doonby Ferness. Come on!" They would take no argument; their mother had given instructions, and that was that.

I was so infected by their excitement, I agreed. The creels were hidden in a clump of whins, I climbed on the garron and they ran me off over the hill.

We stopped by the Findhorn River just the far side of Ferness House, about three miles away. I fell off Dancer, rubbing my bottom, for I wasn't used to riding so fast. We were in a belt of trees near one of the old standing stones. It was leaning sideways over two other stones, overgrown with brambles and some whins, in the middle of a half-acre pasture surrounded by trees. A bonfire was built nearby.

"There it's!" said Aelec. "That's where ye've tae bide."

"Where?" I asked, not understanding.

"There, in under the stane!" he said impatiently. As I gaped, he pulled me over towards it, dodging the snow patches that would show our footprints.

Mag held Dancer, and cried, "Good luck!" Good luck? What on earth was going on?

Aelec carefully opened a path through the brambles for me. Below the stone it was actually quite clear and dry; it stank a bit, and was probably a resting-place for foxes. Still not understanding, I clambered in, tugging my skirts off the thorns, and he pulled the stems up to hide me.

"Now mind you!" he said urgently. "Ye've no' tae let naebody ken ye're in there, ye hear? Jist sit still, watch, an' listen weel. An' never say a word about it, or we're a' dead." I gasped. "We're just in time. They'll be here in a minute, just."

"Who will?" I demanded. "What is this?"

As he turned away towards his sister, he hissed, "Be still! D'ye no' want tae learn how tae ride the kelpie?" His footsteps faded, and I was left crouched uncomfortably among the brambles. Ride the what?

The shadows were growing long already. Although it had been a fine day, there was a good frost in the air, and as

I sat the sweat from the riding chilled on my skin. I grew colder and stiffer every minute. I'd not had anything to eat since dawn, either. Did I want to learn how to – did he really say ride a kelpie? I must have misheard him. This was daft. Maybe they'd just run off with my pony and creels.

I was on the point of climbing back out of my hidey-hole when I heard people moving and shouting in the trees down towards the river. Torches were flickering, and a body of about twenty men were dancing in a kind of procession towards the stones, singing. I knew I couldn't move now.

As I peered out under the stone, through the screen of brambles, I saw with a stab of fear that one of the figures prancing towards me had the head of a horse.

I was frozen. The devil himself was out that night, and I was sure to be found. Oh, gran was right! Why did I ever listen to the gipsies?

The men circled round and round the stones, chanting and waving their torches. I slowly came to realise that they couldn't see me, and when the horse-headed one tripped and swore in the gathering dark, I relaxed just a touch, and started to pay attention. They were only men after all, it seemed.

The singing was strange to me, but after a minute or two I started to pick out a word or two, queerly distorted. It was something about horses, but not any song I knew.

Soon the singing trailed off discordantly. A rough voice shouted out, "Are we a' here? Is a' the Maisters here present?"

They all shouted, "Aye!" waving their torches.

"Aye, then it's time we began, eh? Bring forward the seeker." From the side, where he'd been hidden from me by the stone, a young man, blindfolded, was pushed forward, and stood uncertainly. He was turned to face the stone and all the others gathered round. I felt the stone tremble above me as someone climbed onto it.

"Great Lord o' Horses," the leader shouted, "here is a young man wha earnestly desires for tae be entered in this

Society o' Horsemen, wha by your word hae the maistery o' a' horse-kind. Will ye admit him?"

"Has he been examined?" the man on the stone said from above my head.

"Aye, has he."

"Is he sound in wind an' limb, wi' neither spavin nor splint, ringbone nor strangyles?"

"He is." The men cheered.

"Is he full-grown an' entire, wi' nae vices?" There was a shout or two, suggesting vices that he might have hidden, but they were quickly hushed.

"Is he able tae handle a horse, wi' strength an' will?"

"Aye, he is that. I've teached him mysel', an' he's a good hand wi' any horse I've got i' the yard," said the leader. "He can plough an' harrow, haul timber, drive a cart. He can break a horse easy. I canna complain about him."

"Wha stands for him?" the man above me asked.

"I dae mysel', Jamie Mackenzie, at Ferness, an' Jamie Robb o' Relugas."

"Stan' forward, seeker." The young man cautiously took a step towards me. He was given a candle in one hand and a book in the other, and made to kneel.

"Dae ye earnestly seek entry intae this Society?"

"I dae that." The voice was trembling slightly with nerves, but it was familiar. Where had I heard it before?

"Dae ye swear that when ye learn the Word, that gies mastery ower any an' every horse, ye will never let it pass yer lips where it can be heard by any other livin' soul? No' yer closest friend, no' yer blood brother, no' yer ain wife in the bed beside ye? Dae ye swear that if ye betray the secrets o' this assembly, by choice or chance, ye should be trampled or torn by the first horse that ye meet?"

"I dae."

"Swear it!"

"I swear it."

"Swear on yer hope o' heaven an' yer fear o' hell, on the Book an' the Candle."

"I swear."

"Swear by salt an' bread an' the iron knife." A gobbet of bread was torn off a loaf, dipped in salt, and held on a knife-point at the lad's mouth.

"Swear by fire an' water." A torch, flaring in the wind, was held before him, and his hand was passed swiftly through the flames, and dipped in a bowl of water.

"Swear by sun, wind, rain an' snaw, by yer mother's hearth-stane, by the roots o' yer very soul, that ye'll rip out yer ain tongue afore ye let this secret loose! If any soul learns it from ye, ye'll tak' knife tae them tae keep the tryst. Swear it!"

"Swear!" growled all the men around, swaying forward. I came near to swearing myself, held as I was by the power of the hollow voice above me.

There was a perceptible pause before the young man spoke. "I swear it," he said, his voice shaking.

"Tak' off the cloth an' let him see." As the blindfold was removed, the lad jumped with shock. The man above me leaped down with a yell, which was taken up by all the others; it was the figure wearing the horse's head.

The ceremony went on for a good while, but it grew just into horse-play and drunkenness. There was a carry-on with a horse-collar and bridle, and the lad driven round the field stark naked, like a horse. But at last, as I crouched shivering, aching and wondering how long this would go on and what good I was supposed to get from it, they lit the fire.

They took the lad's clothes and burned them, to get rid of the old smell of a servant of horses, they said. Then, with more ceremony, they led him up to the fire and the horse-headed man presented him with new clothes.

"Wear these free o' all fear o' horse-kind. For now ye are accepted intae the Society o' Horsemen, an' every beast in Scotland will dae yer biddin'. Now come up, an' learn the Words o' Power!" My ears pricked up.

The lad struggled into his new shirt and breeches, and

71

it was only then, as he moved into the firelight, that I recognised him. He was my cousin Iain! What in the world would Aunt Sheila say if she saw him now?

The man in the huge mask called Iain over to the stones and they sat down together not a foot above me. The other men gathered round the fire to pass the bottles round. I could hear what the two beside me said as if they were speaking directly to me.

"There's twa things ye must hae, to be a horse-maister. That's the bane an' the word. Ye hae tae get the bane yersel', wi' nae man nor woman seein' ye. First ye find a toad – no' a frog, mind. Ye kill it wi'out a wound; drown it or burn it in the oven, like. Then ye get a' the banes out o't. Tak' them every ane doon tae a pure spring an' throw them in, carefu' like. Watch what ye're at, an' keep yer eye on them, for ane o' the banes willna sink. Ye lift oot the ane as floats, an' keep it safe in a baggie round yer neck. Whiles ye wear it, ye can speak tae any horse i' the land. Ye'll understan' it, an' it'll understan' ye.

"But the word tae mak' them obey ye is the other thing ye learn, an' mind what ye've sworn, tae keep it secret. The word is this; 'Sic volo'. Ye'll mind it. 'Sic volo'. Ye say that in the lug o' any horse, wi' the bane round yer neck, an' it'll dae yer biddin'."

"'Sic volo'," whispered Iain. "'Sic volo'." And I repeated it silently under the stone.

"Aye. Now ye hae it a'. An' I can tak' aff this bliddy head." With a sigh of relief, the man lifted the heavy mask off his shoulders and laid it on the stone. "Come awa' an' hae a drink, Maister Horseman!" he said jovially, clapping Iain on the back, and the two of them went over by the fire to join the rest. They were greeted with shouts and cheers, and sat down among the group.

The horse-head man was the gipsy who had sold Mistress Clark her dog; or rather, who hadn't sold it.

Well! What a night! I stretched my cramped limbs as far as I could, now that there was no-one near, and tried to take in what I had learned. I could make a magic bone, and I knew the magic word. But if anyone found out – what would they do? Would they really kill me, as the oath said? Aelec had said so, too. Ach, surely not. But would the magic work on a kelpie anyway – even if I could find one? I needed time to consider this.

Suddenly I looked up, as a shadow came between me and the fire. My head bumped on the stone above me, and I gasped with the pain. The shadowy figure jumped, and leaned over the stones to look carefully into the dark below them. I cowered, terrified.

"Wha's that?" I heard Iain's voice, and peered up to see him lifting his head to call the others to catch the spy.

"Iain! It's me! Jeannie!" I whispered frantically, and luckily he caught the name before he shouted. He turned back. No-one had noticed.

"Who? My God, Jeannie! What are ye daein' in there? Dae ye no' ken what's goin' on the night? God Almighty, they'll kill ye, Jeannie! Ye wee idiot!"

So it was true! What was he going to do? Betray me? Or break the oath he had just now sworn?

Somebody shouted to him to hurry up, he was missing his turn at the bottle, and he called back he'd be in just a minute. He leaned over the stone again. "Ye bide there an' dinna budge," he murmured. "I canna tell them – ye're my ain blood. But if ye tell a soul ye've been here, an' seen what ye've seen – an', my God, heard what ye've heard – ye'll get me killed as weel as yersel'. Ye understan'?"

"I'll no' say a word, Iain, I promise," I whispered.

"Aye," he muttered, "an' I've sworn. But what else can I dae?" The men shouted again, and with a final, urgent whisper of, "No' a single word, mind! I'll see ye again!" he lifted the mask and returned to the group.

I curled up in my plaid and lay like a winter hedgehog, growing colder and colder, until at last they finished the drinking and stumbled off through the trees again. By that time I was so stiff I could scarcely rise when Aelec and

Mag came to help me out. They shoved me up on Dancer's back, tied me onto the packsaddle, for I couldn't hold on by myself, and led me gently back through the starry night to granda's house. The folk there were still awake, worried about me. I told them I'd had an accident and the gipsies had helped me, and they thanked them and put me to bed in the warm hay beside the cow, clucking over me like hens that have hatched a gosling.

In the morning, I still told them nothing. I couldn't risk getting Iain into trouble, as well as myself. But I promised myself I'd soon find a toad.

THE
HIGHLANDERS

I was lucky. I hadn't looked forward to killing a poor wee toad, even if it was for my dad's sake, but the next week I fell over a stone by the path and found a dead one underneath, with not a mark on it. I didn't know how it died, frozen maybe, for the weather had suddenly turned to dreadful snow and sleet, but I wrapped it loosely in a scrap of cloth, to be sure not to lose any of it, and buried it in an anthill by the river, for the ants to clean it for me. Hard digging it was in the frozen ground.

What I had forgotten, of course, was that ants die off in winter. Every time I dug it up to check it, it was exactly the same. The cold preserved it. After a while, I let it be.

For some weeks, I was scared of my shadow. I didn't know what that big gipsy man might do if he found out that I'd heard his secrets; there were five of us in danger; me, Iain, Margaret Davidson who had told me of the meeting, Mag and Aelec who knew of it. But as time passed, the fear faded.

With the bare possibility now that I might be able to ride the beast, I started to look for a kelpie in earnest. I bothered my granda Mackay every time I was at the croft about how to find one, till he started asking why I was so interested – and of course I couldn't tell him. I asked the fisher wives on our way out, and they told me no' to be so daft-like, there wasna sic a thing – they hoped. I even girded

75

up my courage and asked the minister, Alexander Rose himself. He took a stick to me, for impertinence, and went down to my parents – the first time he'd been down to the fisher town in three years – to complain about my interest in this heathen rubbish. I had a hard time explaining that away to my mam and the mistress.

I had no luck at all. Nobody knew anything.

And all the time dad just lay there. He was maybe a bit better; his back didn't pain him quite so much, and he could be moved up into the box bed at night. He could help himself with his arms, so that the nursing was that much easier. He started trying to work, mending nets across his knees, and baiting lines, but that was a task for old men and women, and he was slow. It was pitiful to see him, propped up against a folded mattress to hold his back, wrestling slowly and painfully with the work even Ellen found so simple, wincing every time he had to stretch or reach out, or the hooks tore his unaccustomed fingers. And he snarled up the lines badly; they had to be laid just so in the barrels, to lift out free without catching, and dad hadn't the knack. Johnnie never told him how Duggie sneered or beat him for the tangles.

However, we soon had more to think about. The Highlanders arrived.

We knew they were coming, of course. They'd taken Aberdeen near a month before, but were going back to the shelter of the Highlands to gather more men, it was said. Master Clark declared that it was the first time he'd ever heard of a victorious army retreating; for they'd beaten the King's men at every battle. They had been only a hundred miles from London, and the King packing to flee. But then, Highlanders always did things backwards. What the most of us thought was that they'd taken too many cattle from the fat lands of England, and wanted to take back all their loot, so they forced the Rebel Prince to turn back. The Stewarts were a misfortunate family always.

Anyway, from Aberdeen they'd moved north and west.

They attacked Fort William and Fort Augustus, and scared the King's men so that Lord Loudon, King George's general in the North, scuttled away up to Helmdale with a sore tailbone when the Countess of Moy and half a dozen ghillies shouted at him, and he thought it was a whole army – it was the laugh of the country. And then they spread right across from Inverness to Elgin, seeking food like a plague of locusts.

We were in the middle.

There was little sign of all the booty that folk spoke of when the first of them arrived in Nairn. On the fifth day of April a ragged group of forty or so Macdonalds came running into the town by the west road, with two men on horseback in their midst. I was shivering, chatting to my friends by the well, when we saw them stopping by the Horologe Stone. One unslung a set of bagpipes from his shoulder, and they formed themselves into a kind of column to march in, up to the Provost's Town House.

Many of the folk from up the country wore the kilt, and we all had our plaids. Most women had tartan skirts, and some of the men had tartan coats and breeches, though plain grey was just as common. But none of the local people wore these huge tartan philabegs, like ragged blankets wrapped round and round the body and held up only by a belt and a pin on the shoulder. Besides, nearly all our men, and some of our women too, had hose and shoes. These great smelly ruffians were bare-legged in the slush, their teeth yellow in their shaggy beards, their long hair lank round their shoulders, their broadswords and muskets like bairns' toys in their knobby red hands.

We stood and watched silently as the men on horseback drew rein, looking round them. They were dressed in coat and breeches in a civilised way, but how could any sensible person trust himself near those savages? One was about thirty, with lace at his chin like the master on a Sunday. He looked tired and bad-tempered, and needed a shave. The other was a lad of about sixteen, in a green suit with black

77

frogging. He had no lace, but his linen was fine enough – though it needed a good wash.

As they went into the Town House, where Rose of Kilravock lived when in Nairn, I thought to myself I'd best go and tell the master, so I pushed through the crowd that was growing every second, and ran home with the pail splashing. But they had heard already, and the master was bonneted and coated, with the mistress trying to make him put his plaid over his coat to keep off the cold.

"Away wi' ye, wife!" he cried, flapping his arms at her like a hen. "Would ye have me appear before they rapscallions wrapped up like a bairn? I am a Bailie o' this town, an' I'll dress like one."

"An' catch your death!" she snapped back. But it was no use, he shoved past her and headed for the door just as a scared wee quean arrived to say he was to go to the Town House at once. "For the Bailies is tae get their orders aff the officers, sir!"

"Orders! What's the town comin' to, to take orders from a parcel o' red-shanked Irish? Aweel, I'd best be away." He took a deep breath to steady himself, and let it out with a gasp as his wife pulled his head down and kissed him on the cheek. The mistress! "Ach awa', wife!" he muttered. "In front o' the lassies!"

"In front o' the whole town, Patrick Clark," she said proudly. "On ye go, now. An' take as much care as ye can."

As he left, red-faced but heartened, the wee quean trailing at his heels up to the High Street, we heard some shouting, and a single clash of steel, but it soon stopped. Celia and I wanted to go out and watch, but the mistress forbade it. Then she looked at us consideringly, closed the door over, and called everyone into the kitchen.

"There's things to be said here an' now, before any trouble starts that we can avoid. Hugh, you an' Henny will do all the marketin' – supposin' there's still a market – whiles the rebels are in the town. I dinna want any o' the women o' the house goin' out unless it's necessary. An' ye'll take care

78

to be civil an' quiet, Hugh, an' you too, ye wee devil. Ye're like to be fair provoked. Mind now, these are tired, edgy, fightin' men, an' wild Hielanders at that, an' their tempers will be short. You keep out o' their way, an' dinna argue, whatever they do. We can replace anythin' they take or break; we canna replace you. Go an' close the shutters – there's no sense showin' them what we have in here.

"Now, Amanda, ye'll stay in at all times." Amanda looked annoyed. "If I need to send a lass out, I'll send Celia or Jeannie. A wee lass is safer than you would be. An' ye'll stay away from the windows, too." Amanda smoothed her long, fair hair rather smugly. "We've still got good stores, that'll put us by till they're away."

"Mistress," I said, "are they no' likely to claim provisions from us? We'd maybe do well to split up what we have into three or four wee-er stores, an' hide some, or they'll could leave us wi' naethin'."

"That's sense, Jeannie," she said, nodding. "Can ye think o' anythin' else?" She was like that – ready to give credit where it was earned, and take advice if it was going.

"I canna think just now, mistress – just what Mag said once." She made an encouraging noise, and I went on rather doubtfully, "If there's more than ye can fight, then smile or cry an' see can ye talk yer way out, an' ye'll maybe get off wi' little harm: but if there's but the one man, ye can try an' fight him, an' dae whatever ye need to, to get away. Ye can grab him by the –"

"That's good advice, Jeannie," she interrupted firmly, raising one eyebrow – a trick she had. Celia was near giggling, and Amanda was trying to look shocked. "Ye can tell us later what else she told ye. Now, let's get at the stores."

We worked for near two hours before the master returned. Mistress Clark was so relieved to see him back safe, she might have kissed him again, but he was in a tearing hurry.

"I canna stay, Janet. What's that ye're at? Aye, good, keep at it. Hugh, saddle up for me. I've to go an' see can I help some o' their wounded men."

"No, Patrick!" she exclaimed. "They're rebels! It's treason! Ye're puttin' your neck in a noose!"

"From the daughter o' Rose o' Broadley, that's a laugh!" he said, giving her a hug. It must have been the danger that made them so loving. "Your father's the great man in the town the now, that close wi' the Highlanders."

"Ach, Father!" she snapped in disgust. "Who heeds him? But the Prince canna win, surely, an' after they're awa' -"

"No, it's a' right. I'm doin' it under duress, an' I've a letter off the Provost himsel' sayin' they've threatened my life, an' givin' me leave tae go. Hand me my plaid, Jeannie, there's a good lass. There'll be about a thousand men in the town in the next two hours, Janet, an' they'll be spread among the houses. They say they'll pay for what they take, but I dinna ken what with – they havena been paid since they left England. There was supposed to be a ship comin' from France with gold for the Prince, but I'm hearin' she's lost in the Pentland Firth. Bad water, that. Where's my bag? Aye, thank ye, Celia. Now mind – dinna cause trouble, an' we'll maybe no' have any. I must get awa'. Take care, now!" And he was away.

"A thousand men!" Mistress Clark was dumbfounded. "My God!"

In fact, there was very little trouble. The Highlanders were mostly quiet-behaved, and the Nairn folk kept their counsel. A few stones were thrown, a few girls got themselves kissed accidental-on-purpose, two or three heads were broken, and every hen, duck, goose or pig in the town vanished within two days. Mam's was long ago eaten, of course. There was a raid on Danny Souter the cobbler's shop, and all his hides were lifted to make brogans, except the best ones that he'd well hidden, while he lay in his bed and listened to them in the shop below, and never let on he heard; and some other shops were emptied, but on the whole things were quiet. The Provost and all the other Bailies who had houses in the country moved out to them, and left their town houses to the Highlanders.

We had three officers and about ten men, and Amanda, Celia and I moved to sleep on pallets in their parents' room. You couldn't move in the kitchen for glowering, suspicious Highlanders and their smelly philabegs, until the mistress lost her temper and cleared them all out to the stable. How could she cook, she demanded, if she tripped over big deerskin brogans every time she turned round? So they had their meals taken out to them. Having the Gaelic made me the most popular quean in the town, after some were sick the first day, with eating well on an empty stomach, and I managed to convince them they hadn't been poisoned by the pepper in the stew. I was asked to interpret in a dozen houses.

Two of our hidden stores of food disappeared as if by magic. The mistress was fit to be tied.

The Prince himself passed through the town twice, in his carriage with the royal arms painted on the door, but I didn't see it. Few cheered him, I heard. The second time he stopped by at the Town House for an hour or two, and the Bailies were called in. The mistress, in a great pother, put on her best gown to meet him, but he had a streaming cold and didn't stay. She was furious again. When we asked the master about him, he looked grave. "He's a fine, romantic figure of a prince," he said, "but I dinna see a king in him. A king would never have let them turn him back from Derby."

The Prince's chief adviser, Lord George Murray, was about more often, and I saw him once or twice in the High Street. But I had little enough to do with the Highlanders outside.

Then word started coming in of the Duke of Cumberland, the son of King George the Second. He was the commander-in-chief of the King's men, and was coming up from Aberdeen with two other generals and an army. Excitement rose in the town. The Highlanders grew restless, and the townsfolk cocky, and there was a bit more trouble.

Master Clark was still seeing to the sick men. They had frostbite, he said, or scurvy from not eating as they should.

They were half starved, most of them. He had great arguments with the officers billeted on us, about who was the real King. He said it was King George; but they claimed the throne rightly belonged to James, son of the old King James that was put off the throne forty years before for being a Papist. Prince Charles, they said, was come to claim his father's crown for him.

I didn't understand the half of what they were saying. I kept quiet, as the mistress had told us, served their ale and food, and got on with my work. I wasn't like Miss Amanda, making big eyes at the handsome captain, when her mother wasn't watching; and the other older one was too wild for me; but I talked a fair bit with the lad, the young one who had come in with the first men.

His name was Gillies, Alistair Gillies. His father was a draper in Perth, and he had joined to be with his cousin, a tacksman, or tenant, of one of the Macdonald chiefs. It was meant to be a great adventure, he said; the fight against a Foreign Tyrant, the White Cockade, the Loyal Few rising for the True King, home from exile. But it wasn't like that in the end. He was sickened by the war. Not so much the fighting, for he'd seen great courage and heroism, and it was more or less what he'd expected; but the sheer waste and stupidity of it.

One night, sitting by the dying fire, he told me how many of the clansmen had been driven out to join their chieftains, by threats to have their houses burned over their heads, or their cattle killed.

"It wisna fair, Jean," he said dolefully. At times he sounded so young, I felt like his grandmother. "They wis forced out, an' now they're slippin' awa' hame, for they're no' fed nor paid nor naethin'." He spoke with a queer Southron twist. "If the King's men catch them, they'll be hangit as rebels, an' if their ain chiefs catch them, they'll be hangit as deserters, an' if they dinna gang, they'll starve, for their fields'll no' be sown." He sighed.

"Serve them right," I said. "Ye're papists."

"No' all o' us," he said. "An' whit dis it matter onyway? We're only men. I've seen good an' bad in a' kinds o' men these last months."

This idea that papists were ordinary people was a new one to me. My gran said they had horns and a tail and ate babies. The master and mistress were strong against them, too, and approved the laws in some places that hurt them, stopping them getting wed or owning land or even educating their own children. Mam and dad never spoke like that, though, now that I thought about it. And I could see, looking at poor Alistair, sitting in his drawers by the fire while I darned his breeches, that at least the tail bit was wrong, so maybe the rest was, too.

"Are ye Christians?" I asked.

"Of course we are!" he said, insulted. "Dae you no' ken onythin'?"

"But ye're idolators an' bow down afore the Roman Antichrist," I said.

"Eh?" He grinned. "Tell me," he said, "what's an idolator?"

I looked at him rather blankly. I'd never thought to ask. "That's what my gran says," was all I could think to say. He shrugged. "Well, ye hae priests," I said.

"You hiv ministers. It's the same thing."

I didn't know enough to argue. But I went to my bed that night with a new idea to consider. Could Papists be human? It was an unsettling thought, but interesting.

The next day, the twelfth of April, a Saturday it was, I went out down to see my mam and dad. The mistress sent them a bag of meal, and since he wasn't needed by his captain, Alistair came with me to carry it. Just as well he did.

The High Street was almost deserted, in spite of all the men billeted in the town. They were taking so much in tolls from any trader – half the catch from a boat, it was fair ruinous – that nobody was bringing anything in. The boats wouldn't even have gone out if the Rebels hadn't threatened to shoot any fisher that refused. The Friday market was only the quarter of what it should be, and on that Saturday I saw only two women with fish and one with some old onions for sale.

We walked down, saying little. I got on with my knitting, as usual – it was a rare thing to see any woman going about without her needles twittering, if she had a free hand at all. We had a leather pad on a belt at our waists, and stuck one needle into it for support, so that we could knit one-handed, even under the shelter of our plaids. Many a pair of hose I'd knitted for my dad on the way up to the croft.

Down the brae, past the bridge-end, and on down towards the sea. The sleet had stopped, for once. As we came level with the first fisher houses, we heard shouting. "That's my mam!" I said, starting to run. Alistair hefted up the bag of meal on his shoulder and followed, stumbling on the uneven path.

There was a knot of folk before our house. Several of the fisher wives and some men were there, shouting angrily and waving fists and sticks. Some at the back were picking up stones to throw. I wriggled through, to find a dozen or so Highlanders by the step, and two just coming out of the house. A woman was putting a bundle up on her head, a man was leading out Dancer.

Horrified, I jumped forward, like a fool. "What are ye at?" I yelled. "That's our garron! Ye Hielan' thieves, leave him alane!" I tried to pull the rope out of the man's hands, but he pushed me backwards.

One of the others pulled me to my feet, laughing, and slung me across to a third. "Hold the little vixen, Brian!" he called in the Gaelic. "She'll eat us all up else!"

"This vixen will be ripping the throat from you if you don't leave our garron alone!" I screeched, struggling like a mad thing. After all the tellings I'd had about not causing trouble, too! As they stared, surprised that someone could speak the tongue, I managed to drag a hand free and stabbed the man gripping me with my knitting needles. He let me go, cursing. I backed off towards the door, the bone needles held like a knife in front of me, while the rest of them fairly roared with laughter at the pair of us.

Mam came stumbling out of the door, holding the side of her face. She'd been fighting, too. She had a great red weal on her cheek, and the beginnings of a dreadful black eye. Gran and the twins were wailing inside the house, and I could hear dad swearing and shouting from his pallet. I was near spitting blood with rage.

"Leave us be!" mam shouted at them. "Ye thieving scoundrels, why can ye no' let honest folk alane?" A fine roasting we gave them – but suddenly I was seized from behind. I screamed.

One woman had crept in the stable door, through the house, and gripped me from the back. She held my hair with one hand and twisted my wrist with the other till I had to drop the needles. Then she held me out to her cheering friends, and called, "Who is wanting a fine red fox-skin to warm his fingers, eh?"

I writhed, yelling as the hair started to tear from my scalp. Mam hit out at the Highland wife, but there was no strength in her arms. Our neighbours in the crowd were shouting, but the threatening broadswords held them back.

Suddenly there was silence. It was a moment before I realised I'd heard a pistol shot. Into the quiet dropped a voice I scarce recognised. "Is this the way the Chisholms treat their own people?" There was a stillness. Alistair had arrived.

They looked at him in doubt. The hand in my hair slackened the least bit.

"What is going on here? " There was still silence. "I am Ensign Alistair Gillies, of Macdonald of Glengarry's Regiment. Who is in charge here?"

One of the men stepped forward. "We have orders from Roderick Og MacIan his own self, to be finding horses to carry the sick. These are not our people, Alistair Gillies, or they would be offering their garron willingly to the Prince's service."

"When you mistreat their women, there seems little reason why they should," said Alistair. He seemed all at once far more grown-up than he'd been the night before. The woman holding me released me, and I went to support mam. Dad and the others were quiet in the house, listening.

"Mistreat them?" called out the man I had stabbed, holding out his hand with the blood still dripping from the fingers. "It's them that's mistreating us, I'm thinking!" They laughed, rather uneasily.

"Would you not wish your own wives and daughters to defend your property? Then you cannot complain if others do the same. And is that bundle also a horse?" Alistair's Gaelic was not quite correct, but quite clear in its meaning.

"It's my man's clothes, an' a' the blankets!" mam said.

"Had you orders to take that too?" asked Alistair. "To steal from a cripple? No? Then put it down."

The woman dropped the bundle reluctantly. Alistair turned to my mam and spoke in English, so that the crowd could understand.

"Mistress Main, these men takin' your garron are but daein' their duty to their ain clan. We hiv sick men wha must be moved. It's hard on you, I ken, but there's naething I can nor will dae to stop them." There was an angry mutter from our friends, but the Highlanders nodded approvingly. "I'll speak to Roderick Og this day," Alistair went on," an' see will he pay for the garron. If he disna, I'll dae it mysel'."

There were still angry looks about in plenty, but the worst of the hostility was fading. As the Highlanders, with even a word of apology to me, led poor Dancer off up the path, there was no more than a curse or two thrown at them, instead of a stone.

"We are most grateful, sir," said mam. She was still holding her head, but looked less shaken. "Will you no' come in an' take a cup o' tea?" She led Alistair into the house, where he greeted my dad and gran politely, as if there had been no trouble outside.

I followed, rubbing my head and shaking from reaction. I didn't feel so grandmotherly now. It was more like in church; I couldn't take my eyes off him. I'd cheerfully have died for him.

Suddenly I remembered the meal, but when I dived out to get it, it was gone. The Highlanders must have lifted it. My needles were there, though, with the sock still on them. It was aye something.

THE TEST

As everyone expected, the Highlanders moved away soon. Alistair himself left on the next day, the Sunday. We all went to the Kirk in the morning, as usual, and when we were coming home I saw Alistair with about ten of his men standing outside the Tron. Without waiting for permission, I ran over to him, ignoring the scandalised hisses of the mistress behind me.

Arrived in front of him, with everyone looking, I scarce knew what to say. "Is that ye awa', then, Alistair?" I asked at last. I didn't want him to leave. Had he not saved me from the Chisholms the day before, and paid mam for Dancer? I desperately wanted him to stay. But he looked down at me with a smile.

"Aye, Jeannie, we're aff in a meenit. Here, there's somebody here I want you to meet. Father Malcolm, this is the lassie in the surgeon's hoose. Jeannie Main." It was a priest! I'd have run in horror, but my legs wouldn't have carried me. Then I took thought to myself, and looked again. He wore a long black dress. Maybe Gran was part right, and it was just priests had tails.

He smiled at me from about six feet up, and his thin brown face was kindly. "Good day to you, Mistress Jean Main," he said. "Alistair here tells me you were in a pickle yesterday."

At the third try, "Aye, sir, an' he saved me," I managed to gasp out.

He grinned at Alistair. "You've made a friend here, I see, my son. You're not of our faith, Jean? Ah, well, bless you anyway, my child, and God keep you out of trouble in future. God can work miracles, eh?"

About the tail, I decided probably not. He turned away, but I made bold to touch his gown. "Aye, lassie, what is it?"

I had suddenly thought, if he was a Highlander, maybe he could tell me where and how to find a kelpie. But he shook his head, with a roar of laughter. Amanda was staring. The master and mistress were pretending not to watch. "Bless you, child, I haven't laughed like that in a long time. No, my dear, I do not know anything about kelpies. Why is it so important?"

"Oh, nothin', sir," I muttered, red-faced. Would I never learn – making an exhibition of myself in front of the whole town, talking with a Papist priest! That gipsy was right trouble.

He studied my face thoughtfully. "Well, Jeannie, whatever it is, I'll pray that you find what you seek. On you go now, or your mistress will be very angry." True for him.

Just at that moment the captain rode by. He was on Master Clark's horse! It seemed it wasn't just the poor folk who lost their ponies. The Macdonald waved to Alistair to follow. The priest moved off, and Alistair swung into his saddle. He reached down and took my hand. "Cheerio, Jeannie," he said. "Dinna forget me, eh?"

"Na'," I sniffed, trying not to cry. I was certain I'd never see him again.

He suddenly bent down in the saddle and kissed my hand. "Here noo, here noo. Gie us a smile, Jeannie love. I'll be back some day, I promise." I sniffed even harder, and tried to smile as he wanted. He slipped something down into my hand, sat up suddenly and shouted to his men to come away. As he rode off up the High Street, his men trotting after him, he never looked back.

I felt that every eye left in the town was on me, and I didn't care. I just ran to the house, where I hid in the stable. I couldn't bear folk round me.

They left me alone, on the mistress' own orders. That afternoon, when I finally came out, she didn't say a word. Henny was grinning, of course. Amanda glowered – she was maybe jealous – and dear Celia had saved me a piece of shortbread to cheer me. But it was a while before I could feel easy with them again.

The thing in my hand was a shilling. I hid it away safe.

The master was worried in case the Duke of Cumberland's army would have to fight for the town, but he had no need. When the Duke's scouts and cavalry came near the bridge on the Monday, there were only a few dozen Rebels left in Nairn. Frenchies, they were, mostly, and Irish. They fired some shots, to show a bit spirit, and rode out at a canter, with the jeers of the Nairn folk after them, and a few stones thrown. And the Duke of Cumberland rode in.

Everybody cheered him. Except me. I didn't know whose side I was on any more. I didn't know what was wrong with me.

The Duke's men set up a proper camp, at Balblair House, just outside the town to the south. The cannon, huge monstrous things I thought them, stayed on the east of the bridge, safe from any Rebel attack. I was busy washing, for the mistress stripped and changed the beds the Rebel officers had slept in. Wise she was, for that night we had another three officers, of Barrell's Regiment. There was a big fat one, a little fat one, and a tall, thin one. The youngest was the thin one, a Major Wolfe, and he was near thirty. I missed Alistair.

Mind you, that Major Wolfe was a nice enough fellow. He was shy, and kept twisting off his buttons while he was trying to think what to say. He gave me a penny that afternoon for sewing them on firm for him. If this war went on, I'd end up rich.

The master had a sharp interview with the Duke himself, to clear himself of any charge of dealing with the rebels. But he showed Provost Rose's letter, and that was all right. Cumberland could scarce refuse to accept the Provost's letter when he was staying, like the Rebels before him, in the Provost's house.

The town was fair buzzing that day, and half the night. All the people came out, the first time for weeks, and took the air – though the weather was still very cold, at least they knew they'd be safe from robbers. It was like a fair day, almost, though there wasn't much left in the town to sell. Christian Sutherland and the other alewives had their best day in a month. It was well after midnight when the last roisterer left the street quiet, and I could get to sleep, wondering where – or if – Alistair was sleeping.

Next day, Cumberland's men had a rest day. It chanced to be the Duke's birthday, and he gave them all an extra ration of bread, cheese and brandy to celebrate it, and after their hard march from Aberdeen, a day to mend their uniforms. We could hear the bands playing as they paraded and drilled, but they still had time to come into the town. The Merrieton girls unstitched the white bows they had put on for the Prince's men, and made fresh ones in red and yellow, for the Duke. Peter Falconer the smith was working, mending harness, from the Taptow drum till after sunset. He'd hidden while the Rebels were in town, for fear of being kidnapped to serve them, as had happened to other smiths, and was glad to be out again. That day too, the alewives did brisk business, and many of the hill farmers brought in sheep and cattle they'd saved from the Highlanders, to sell to the army sutlers. One or two folk that had saved their hens let them out, and quickly regretted it; the women of this army were as thieving as the last one.

Ships were arriving in the Firth all day, anchoring just off the river bar, and sending in boatloads of provisions, and officers, men and horses to the Duke. There was a regiment there, Houghton's, I think, that was just newly arrived from the Americas, and some Hanoverians – fine, polite big men, though they had little English – and even the dour Nairn folk were excited and interested.

But there was a grim side to all this busyness. The word went round in the morning that a lad had been caught spying for the rebels, and was to be tried and hanged. I thought sad for the lad, and got on with the ironing.

The minister called, to see the master, who was out. Miss Amanda invited him to wait in the parlour, and take a glass of claret with her and the big fat officer, who was off duty at the time. You couldn't have stopped him with any two regiments in the town. After a while, they began playing music, with the English officer teaching them the newest London song, 'God Save the King'.

I was ironing sheets, and one of the officers' servants, that they called a batman, was peeling potatoes – more serviceable than the Highlanders, they were – and playing with the spit dog. Their names were similar, Dandy and Andy, and the man had taken a right fancy to the snappy wee brute. He was trying to teach it to jump through a hoop of his arms, with some danger to his nose and a great deal of laughter from Celia and myself, when there was a knock at the door. Celia came back open-eyed to tell me, "It's that gipsy wife. With the one ear."

Margaret Davidson, in the town itself? It must be important. Well, the Englishman, Andy, wouldn't know he should tell the Bailies. "Bring her in, then," I said, putting down the iron on the hearth. Luckily the mistress was out, and Amanda busy. "What can I be doing for you, Mistress Davidson?" I asked, setting a chair for her. She had both her earrings in the one ear, and smiled as she saw Celia staring.

"Fine manners in a fine house. I said that to your mother two year by, an' it's still true," she said. "Ye've heard the news?"

"Which news?" I asked. There was so much going on.

"The lad that's to be hanged up at Balblair. Ye ken about him?"

"Well, we know he's to be tried – " Celia said.

"It's decided. He's for hangin'. But dae ye ken who he is?" We looked blank. "I telt ye, did I no'? We'd meet in the shadow o' the gibbet. It's your cousin. Iain. Aye, this is the second time."

"Iain?" I almost screamed. Celia jumped a foot, and Henny stuck his nose in the door from the stable, but I paid no attention. "Are ye sure, Mistress?"

"Certain sure," she said. Henny's ears were flapping, and his malicious little eyes were bright.

"Oh, God, what can I dae?" I gasped. I knew I must do something. My own cousin! And he'd risked his own life at the secret meeting, rather than betray me. I had to do something. What? What?

"Ye'll help him. It's your fate, lass. Aye." She rose and moved elegantly to the door. "Ye're mindin' on the kelpie?"

"Tae the Devil wi' a' kelpies!" I snapped. "If Iain's in the hands o' the King's men, what can I dae? The Duke wouldna see me."

"That's true, lovey," said Andy. "There ain't nobody what'll listen to a little lass."

"What can I dae?" I demanded, frantic.

"Naethin'," said the gipsy. As I turned angrily away, furiously helpless – what can a child do in a man's world? – she went on, "Naethin' yersel', but whocould help ye, eh? Think on it. Ye need help. Who is there?"

"The master!" It was all I could think of.

"He's out at David Cumyng's, about the fever on the ships," Celia said.

"Send for him," the gipsy said.

"Send? For the master? I couldna order him about."

Henny's narrow wee face lit up with mischief. He saw how he could get me into trouble, with no risk to himself. "I'll go an' fetch him," he squeaked. "I'll say ye sent me to tell him to come at right awa'." And he jinked out the door. He knew fine the master would be angry, getting orders from a serving lass, in front of the new Depute Sheriff. But I was past caring for that.

"He'll be ower late," Margaret Davidson said. "I but learned a few minutes bye mysel'. The hangin's set for noon. Na', ye need somebody nearer."

"You could ask Major Wolfe, but 'e's up at the camp," the Englishman said. He seemed quite interested. "'Im in there wouldn't shift 'is backside to save 'is mother, let alone a Scotchman."

"There's the minister," Celia suggested.

"Master Rose? Oh, no!" I said. "I couldna!"

"What way no?" said the gipsy. "Scared?" She slipped out the door.

"There's nobody else," Celia urged me. "Go on, you have to try."

"Can't lose nothin', love," said Andy. Little he knew! He nodded encouragingly.

With knees trembling, I approached the parlour door. I had to try twice before I could bring myself to knock on it. The last time I'd seen the minister, he'd tried to wallop me with his stick. He'd likely not do that here, not in front of Miss Amanda and the officer, but if he took offence – the minister was a powerful man. And he disliked me already. A whipping wouldn't matter, but I could be losing my job – and my parents needed the money and food I brought in. But there was nothing else I could do.

"Come in," called Miss Amanda. She'd put by her harp and was sitting by the table in her best brown dress with the lace, a glass of claret by her hand – she was but just allowed it unwatered, being now sixteen and a young lady. The Reverend Rose sat opposite her, the bottle beside his fiddle on the table, and the fat officer was spread over a chair by the fire, playing a flute. He stopped, and they all stared at me. "What is it, Jeannie?" Amanda asked, coldly.

"Oh, miss!" I could scarcely speak. "I'm sorry for breakin' in on you, but I'm needin' help! Will ye please help me, sir! Please! It's my cousin. He's been arrested for spyin', an' he's tae be hanged, an' he'd no' dae a thing like that, sir, an' – "

"Jeannie!" Miss Amanda's voice, that had been cold, was now freezing. "Will you stop snivellin' an' tell the Reverend just what it is you want? I'm sorry, gentlemen," she said to them, as I wiped my eyes on my apron and tried to control myself.

"Don't fret, my dear," the minister answered in his dry snarl. "I know Jean Main of old. Well, Jeannie? What's this about a hangin'?"

His voice was cutting, but I had to go on. "My cousin Iain, sir. They say he's a spy. But I'll swear he's innocent, sir."

"And I've to go an' ask for a pardon for him?" he sneered.

I misunderstood. "Oh, thank ye, sir! They'll listen to a fine gentleman like yoursel'. Thank ye!"

"You have it wrong, my dear. I'll no' set foot before the Duke to ask for any such thing. Imagine, me ask mercy for a traitor? I'd be mad to consider it. And you're mad to ask it. I'd risk the gibbet mysel'."

"'S true for you, reverend," grunted the officer. "Billy's not a kind little man, by George he ain't. Flog you as soon as look at you – sooner, by George! He don't like the Scotch."

I could scarcely believe it – and yet it was what I had expected. I was desperate. "I'm sorry, sir," I said, my hands twisting my apron to floor rags, "but please, will ye no' help? Please? Ye're our only hope."

His little eyes flickered. Deliberately, he poured himself another glass of claret. "I'd have thought a fine, educated lass like yoursel' could have found some means to get your way," he sneered. "Could you no' write the Duke a letter?"

"There isna time, sir." My lips were trembling. I was shaking all over.

"Write?" The officer sat up with a jerk. "She can write? Good God!" He muttered to himself several times, "Write! Servin' sluts writing! By George!"

Reverend Rose frowned at me. "You're a boastful wee besom, Jean Main!" he snapped. "You give yourself airs beyond your station! Write a letter, indeed!"

"I could, sir," I said. I couldn't think straight. He had an egg stain on his coat front, shaped like a hen.

"Oh, you could, could you?" A malicious smirk stretched his lips slightly. "I'll tell you what, Jean. You prove to me that you have been learning, that you can read and write, and I'll see what I can do."

"That's a fair offer, Joan, by George it is," said the redcoat. He took a gulp of his wine, and leaned back again expansively. "A wager, by George! Yes, fair enough."

What could I say? "What – how, sir?"

The minister took down a book at random from the shelf by the mantelpiece, and opened it. "Here," he said, "come and read this."

My eyes blurred as I looked at it. Miss Amanda was frowning, but said nothing. It was one of the master's books, a treatise on the circulation of the blood. I'd been reading it with Celia a month before, but the letters seemed to dance before my eyes. "Too hard, eh? A pity." He looked over at the Englishman and shrugged.

"No – no, sir, I can manage it." I started to read, and the sound of the words steadied me. He sniffed in annoyance as I reached the end of the page, only stumbling a little over the long words. The officer guffawed in surprise.

That was the start of the worst examination any child could hope to avoid. With my cousin's death hanging – almost literally – over me, I had to read, spell, count for him. If I made one mistake, he might take it as proof that I could not do what I'd said. I had to be perfect. And all the time, the Englishman was commenting, sniggering, to the minister and Miss Amanda, about my accomplishments being good enough for a circus, by George they were.

Miss Amanda looked more and more awkward and unhappy. Once or twice she started to interrupt, but Master Rose carried right on.

We finished the counting, and went on to geography. The sweat was trickling down my spine. Then history. French? I didn't learn French. "I'm glad to know there's one area you've decided to leave to your betters."

Then, as the minister, he moved on to the catechism. At eleven, I should know most of it. He started at the beginning. "What is the chief end of man?"

I was on safe ground here. "Man's chief end is to glorify God and enjoy Him forever." I knew all the questions and answers that taught us our religion, right up to the end. I'd been drilled in them since I was three, and I was a quick learner. But there were a hundred and forty-nine of them. He couldn't mean to work right through them all? He did.

We were well on, at "The sinfulness of that estate whereinto man fell consists in the guilt of Adam's first sin, the want of original righteousness, and the corruption of his whole nature, which is commonly called Original Sin; together with all actual transgressions which proceed from it," when the door swung quietly open. As the minister, not noticing, went on to the next question, Miss Amanda stood up abruptly, looking scared. The officer belched, staring in surprise at the master in the doorway, thunderously angry as I had never seen him.

He stepped silently up behind Master Rose, and as the minister, warned perhaps by my face, turned towards him, the master gripped him by his threadbare neckcloth, lifted him and held him up on his toes, hands clawing the air. Master Clark's big hands were trembling, and his face white with fury.

"I couldna credit it. A minister of religion, treating a wee lass like this. Ye're a disgrace to your cloth, sir. A torturing, vile, disgusting imitation o' a man. The Inquisition in Spain could scarce do worse. I could hardly credit what Celia told me. I wouldna hae believed it if

97

I hadna seen it with my own eyes. You – you – " He was shuddering with rage, and I started to cry out of sheer tension.

That seemed to bring the master back to himself. He dropped the minister to his knees, gasping for breath, his face purple. Turning to Miss Amanda, the master said, "You, miss, up tae your room. I'll speak to ye later. Allowin' this abomination to take place in my house!" She fled, a hand to her mouth to stifle her sobs, and the heels of her good shoes clattered up the stair.

The master looked over at the English officer, who was trying to rise from his chair. He spoke clearly, in contempt. "Over you, sir, I have no control. I can but say that if I had, I would see to it that you never came near my house or mysel' again. I would be obliged if you would find other quarters. Your behaviour is such as no civilised man could tolerate. I find you totally offensive."

The Englishman reddened and started to bluster, but the master held the door for him. "Sir," he said, "would you wish me to make this tormentin' of a young lassie known to your fellow-officers?" The man's eyes sank. I saw Andy hiding a wide grin at the kitchen door as the officer, crestfallen, heaved himself up to his bedroom.

Then the master turned to Master Rose again. "Now, sir," he was beginning, when we heard, faintly on the wind, the rattle of side-drums. "What's that?" he said.

Andy stepped forward. "It's the drum for the hangin', sir," he said with a regretful glance to me. "It's too late to do anythin'."

"He's bein' hanged now? Oh, dear God!" I cried.

"As soon as the drums stop, lovey. That's when they'll drop him."

I collapsed on the bottom step, weeping helplessly. But the master wasn't finished yet. He reached out and hauled Master Rose to his feet by the collar of his coat.

"He's no' dead yet!" he snapped. "You'll come wi' me, minister – " he stressed the last word in contempt – "an' keep your bargain. We'll maybe be in time. Run, man, run! Or I'll see you run out o' the town!"

He dragged Master Rose out, up to the High Street and round the corner. But it was a five minute walk to Balblair House, and as they turned out of sight the drums stopped. It was all over.

Celia and Andy both tried to comfort me, but in vain. Mistress Clark's brisk questions and horrified sympathy when she returned helped more. After a few minutes, she whisked upstairs to see Amanda, and the sound of slaps and wailing came down from the bedroom.

Suddenly the drums started again. "Another one?" said Andy in surprise. "I didn't know as 'ow there was two for off today. Must 'ave been a quick trial." The drums stopped, and he sighed. "Another poor devil gone to 'is Maker," he said. "Wonder what 'e done wrong."

I was past caring. I just sat dully, staring at the fire going down. I wondered if I should get the ironing finished. There was still a sheet to do.

Then the drums started a third time.

"Blimey," said Andy. "Fat Billy's celebratin' 'is birthday in style, inn'e? Three on 'em? That's a bit much, even for 'im. Where'd the other two come from?"

A dreadful suspicion came to me. "The master – an' the minister -" I whispered.

"Oh, no!" cried Celia.

He stared at me in amazement. "That's nonsense, lovey – even if they are Scotch. No, they're safe enough. 'E couldn't do nothin' to them."

But the mistress came down the stair, as white as her kerchief, and I could see the same thought in her mind. She took Celia and me in her arms, and we stood in the big kitchen, waiting for news.

MAKE AND BREAK

It was near an hour before word came. Andy had persuaded us to move down by the fire, but the mistress still clutched us, for comfort; whether for her or for us, I couldn't say. At last a tiny drummer boy, only about eight years old, came skidding to a halt at the door, his drum bouncing on his kilt. "Clark?" he shouted importantly. "I am having a message for Clark!"

"'Ere!" called Andy, as the mistress didn't move.

The lad saluted scrappily. "Message begins. Boy safe. Bringing him home soon. Message ends." He saluted again, relaxed a little, and grinned expectantly.

After a moment, Mistress Rose moved stiffly in her chair. Andy looked at her from the door, reached out and pulled the boy in. "Right, Drummer -"

"MacCallum, corporal. Argyll Militia. Colonel Jack." He was one of the Campbell regiment.

"Drummer MacCallum," Andy said, "stand easy an' tell us about it."

"Yess, corporal!" said the boy, moving smartly in beside the fire. It was cold. "Where should I be starting?" His west-coast accent was soft, but his grin was sharp and bright.

"Were that Scotch lad tried?"

"Inteed he wass, corporal, and wass he not found guilty? And then a thing happened that you would not believe unless you had been seeing it." He paused, enjoying our total attention.

"Well, get on with it, yer scut!" said Andy. And the lad told us, in his fractured English, an almost incredible tale.

Iain had been brought out, protesting furiously in the Gaelic, paying no attention to the regimental chaplain praying at his side. He was mounted on a cart tail among the soldiers drawn up to witness the punishment of a traitor, with the Duke of Cumberland himself standing among his officers and aides at the door of Balblair House to watch. The word was given, the horse driven forward; Iain fell, swung for a second, and crashed to the ground as the rope broke.

In the confusion which followed, with the sergeant swearing fit to be splitting' at the corporal of the hanging party and the corporal swearing at the men, Major Wolfe that was billeted on us spoke up for the lad. 'The sentence was he should be hanged, sir, and he has been,' he argued, but his superior officer, General Hawley, disagreed. 'Hanged till he's dead, sir, hanged till he's dead, that was the order. Carry it out!' And with a fresh rope round his neck, Iain was again heaved coughing up onto the cart. Once again, the cart was jerked out from below his feet, and again, to astonishment, anger and some smothered laughter from the soldiers, the rope broke.

As the sergeant, purple in the face, sent for new rope, there was an interruption. Two men shoved in past the distracted sentries, one dragging the other by the collar. They marched across the cobbled yard to where the Duke was standing complaining of the cold. Then the larger of the pair pushed forward the other. 'Get on with it,' he snarled, 'like you agreed!'

The other, the minister, trembled but did as he was told. On his knees where he had fallen before the Duke and his officers, he begged for the life of the lad. Mercy, clemency, forgive them that trespass – but the Duke cut him off short. In his faintly German accent, he refused.

'For if I should grant you this, what do I say to every other man who comes to beg the life of a traitor? No, no, he dies.' 'Quite right, Your Royal Highness,' agreed General Hawley.

By this time a new rope had been found and tested, six men hauling on each end. Iain was lifted up, the noose adjusted, and the third time the cart was driven forward. And this time the rope held. There was a cheer from the soldiers, who wanted to get in out of the cold, and the Duke turned to go in for a glass of port wine to warm him.

But as Iain hung, kicking and spinning, Master Clark pushed the minister forward again. Ignoring the frowns and laughs of the officers, and casting scared looks at the master, he begged again for Iain's life. 'It is Your Royal Highness's birthday,' he said. 'Would it not be a royal and gracious gesture to pardon this one poor lad, to mark the occasion in a way which will make Your Highness's name remembered here with love and respect, instead o' hatred and fear?'

And that finally struck a chord in the Duke. General Hawley argued that birthday or no, fear was what they had come to drill into the Scotch. 'Here, you,' he ordered the sentries, 'kick 'em out!' But the Duke held up his hand. 'On my birthday, yes,' he said thoughtfully. 'It is good to be merciful.'

'Indeed yes, Your Royal Highness,' said Master Rose eagerly, 'And I am assured that the boy is a simple country fellow, only arrested by accident, and truly innocent.'

'And fery, fery lucky, eh, gentlemen?' said the Duke to his aides. 'If we let him go, perhaps some of his luck vill rub off on us. And we may need it tomorrow, eh? You can have him. Better hurry, Major, or he may not be so lucky after all!' And all laughing at the feeble joke, the officers went in, while Major Wolfe shouted to the sergeant.

When the drummer boy had left, Iain was breathing again, and the master and the regimental surgeon were bleeding him, trying to bring him round.

The boy beamed at us. "Indeed," he said hopefully, "the throat on me iss dry with so much speaking."

"Can I give 'im a drink, mam?" asked Andy, as the mistress didn't move.

She slowly unwound her arms from Celia and me. She had been gripping us fiercely for a long time. "Drink?" she said with some difficulty. "Drink? Yes, yes, o' course, Corporal, give the lad something." Andy, with a wink to the drummer, poured out two brimming mugs of ale, and they supped them noisily. Celia and I watched numbly as the mistress lifted my iron hot from the hearth and carefully put it away in the meal bin. We hunted it an hour that night, to finish the last sheet, but only found it next day when I went to make the breakfast bannocks; for we had no recollection of her action.

The drummer boy was given a whole shilling, and trotted off up the street with his grin practically visible round the back of his head.

When the master arrived, with two men carrying Iain on a stretcher, he was surprised by the warmth of his welcome, but we could not explain. I tried to kiss his hand, but he snatched it away, and apologised to me, and insisted that Amanda did so too, in front of everyone, for allowing me to suffer such cruelty. I was as scarlet as she was.

Iain was bedded down in the stable. Round his neck, where the rope had burned and twisted, there were great black and red ridges, dreadful to see. He was not conscious yet, but snoring and coughing from time to time. The master said that he would recover slowly. But he had some bad news for me. He was sorry, he told me, but he couldn't keep Iain in the house. "For the morn, Jeannie, or maybe the day after, there'll be a battle nearby, an' I must keep all my space for the wounded men I'll have to see to then. Your mother can nurse the lad as well as I can. An' there's ship fever on two o' the ships frae the Americas, an' all. It might spread in the town, an' I'll be needed again."

Luckily, mam had heard of the miraculous escape

before she learned that it was her own brother's lad. She was so glad he was safe, she'd have taken in a dozen of him, and gran told me I should go down on my bended knees to thank the Lord for such a master. She was too late – I already had.

That night we heard a word that had every soul in Nairn laughing. While the Duke of Cumberland, King George's son and general, was living in Rose of Kilravock's Town House in Nairn, with warm letters from the laird welcoming him and telling him to treat the place as his own, the wily Rose was hosting the Rebel Prince Charles Stewart in his country house at Kilravock.

Charles had been staying in Culloden House, not far off, and out of pure sport had decided to visit Kilravock Castle. I wish I could have seen Mistress Rose's face when she got the news of her visitor.

The Prince and forty of his men dined, and kissed the children, and jested about the coming day's fight. Mistress Rose, they said, had the vapours when he left, and had to take to her bed with the strain. I'm not surprised. What would the Duke of Cumberland say when they met him?

But now, whichever prince won, Kilravock had entertained him the day before the battle. It was typical of the Roses. You could see how they had kept their place in the country for generations.

That afternoon and evening, every now and again I had a fit of the shivers and the strangest urge to cry at nothing at all. I felt a proper fool. Miss Celia wasn't much better. Eventually the mistress, who was nervous and excited her own self, told us to come away to bed and sleep it off. But I couldn't settle, with the mistress snoring in the high bed, Amanda sniffling and tossing on her pallet on one side, and Celia kicking and muttering on the other. And the streets were noisy still, with roistering soldiers.

After trying for some time to sleep, I decided to get up and make myself a cup of tea. I had hidden a wee store of goodies behind a loose plank in the stair wall, with some tealeaves in it. If I was quiet, I could manage it without disturbing the Englishmen sleeping in the kitchen, and even if I did wake them, they'd not let on to the mistress, if I gave them a cup too.

I crept out of the room and down the stairs, missing the creaky ones, and into the kitchen. The soldiers were sound. I checked on Iain, sleeping in the stable, snoring and grunting by Hugh and Henny. He was my excuse if I was found up. I came back to the kitchen, turned the pot on its swee out over the fire, and fished out my precious tealeaves. If I was caught with them, there would be trouble. As I put a pinch into a cup, and stowed the rest away, I heard a soft tap, tap at the door. Who on earth could it be, at this hour? It was after midnight, for I'd heard the watch go by.

I went to the door, and whispered, "Who is it?" I was somehow sure that it would be Margaret Davidson again, but it wasn't. It was her son Aelec.

My duty was plain. Keep the door shut, tell him to go away, and if he didn't, rouse the master. But a voice spoke in my mind. I did what it said. I eased the door open silently, and he slipped in.

"What d' ye want?" I whispered. If I was found letting in a strange lad like this, a whipping would be the least of it. "Why did you want in?"

He looked round the kitchen at the sprawled bodies of the soldiers, like dead men in blankets all over the floor. "Why did ye let me in?" he countered, with the sly grin he knew enraged me. With all these men around, he knew I couldn't argue or shout.

But I had another trick. I turned away to the fire, and filled my cup with hot water. The scent of the tea spread through the kitchen, making my mouth water. One of the soldiers muttered and sighed, rolled over and slept again. Aelec's black eyes gleamed in the night-light's flicker. "Tell me, an' I'll mak' you a cup too," I offered.

He grinned. "Go ahead," he whispered. "I'll tell ye." I got out another pinch of leaves, feeling him noticing my wee hidey-hole, just out of habit; and made him a cup. Like me, he raided the honey-jar to sweeten it. We sat on our heels in by the still-warm hearth to talk quietly.

"I've been out-bye the moor," said Aelec. He went night-walking often, like all gipsies. They weren't afraid of ghosts, as house folk were, and the night was the best time to find 'stray' hens or 'lost' sheets bleaching on a bush. I wasn't surprised that he had been out to see what profit he could make of the two armies.

"There's a lot doin' the night," he murmured. "The Hielands is spread a' ower Drumossie Moor. That man – Hay, is it? – that's supposed to be in charge o' their feedin' couldna organise a rabbit doon its hole. They've no' ate for twa days, some o' them, an' they're that tired an' hungered the redcoats could stack them like sheaves an' they'd no' stir. Wi' food for them a' lyin' ready in Inverness, an' nae carts tae fetch it. An' they're for tryin' a night attack, the dafties."

"Night attack?" I said. "Where?"

"Sh! On the camp," he whispered. "Here at Balblair. They're comin' in by night, tae attack at dawn. They think the redcoats will be sleepin' sound after their drinkin' the day. They might be right, but I wouldna bet my last shillin' on it. They're like tae be met wi' mair nor they think. It's the Prince's ain scheme, they were sayin'."

I never thought to ask how he knew. He'd probably been sitting under a whin bush, listening to men talking. Silence and stillness was the way he'd been reared. All I could see in my mind was the fighting at Balblair, and men dying there. Maybe Alastair. Maybe Major Wolfe – no, he was asleep up the stair. Being a private kind of man, he'd not been invited to the parties and ale-drinkings that most of the other officers were at, in spite of the likelihood of a battle the next day. Fat Billy's health was being drunk all over town. If the Rebels attacked now –

"Are ye no' goin' tae warn the soldiers?" I asked.

"Whit way?" he said in surprise. "They'd no' believe me, an' if they did, why should I help the King's men?

They never helped a gipsy ever. The Prince is more like to look kindly on tinker folk than King George's men. Na', they can look out for theirsel's. It's their job, after all, nae business o' mines."

"Dae ye think the attack'll succeed?" I wondered.

"How the devil should I ken?" he replied. "I'm no' a soldier, thank God. I wouldna reckon so, mysel', but I'm no expert. There'll be good pickin's anyway. Battles is good for the poor folk that can get in an' lift what's left."

"Rob the dead?" I said uneasily.

"Why no'?" he asked reasonably. "They're deid. They dinna need their boots or watches." Then he chilled me again. "An' if they're no' just deid yet, ye can aye help them on a wee bit, eh?"

"Kill them, you mean? That's murder, Aelec!"

He shrugged, withdrawing behind the gipsy mask. "They're like tae die in the cold anyway," he retorted. Clearly, he saw nothing wrong with robbing dead or dying men, and was angered that I should think to criticise him for it. It was his way of life, harder and tougher than my own. I could see he regretted taking me into his confidence. "I'll be awa' now, Mistress Jean," he said formally. "I thank ye for your kindness." Maybe he saw that I was sorry to have hurt his feelings, for he grinned at me. "An' I'll no' tell Mistress Clark on ye for pinchin' her tea!" he added.

I let him out and locked the door again behind him. As I returned to the kitchen to rinse out the cups, I was wondering what should I do. Tell the soldiers? They'd ask how I knew, and I'd be in trouble – and so would Aelec. And what would happen to Alastair if he was in the attacking army? But then it might happen anyway. Or should I say nothing? Let the attack go ahead, and maybe the Pretender win his crown? But the fighting could spread through the town. My parents and the Clarks on one side, Alastair and avoiding trouble on the other. What should I do?

I turned from the basin and near jumped out of my skin.

One of the blanketed figures on the floor was sitting up, eyes shining. The cups slipped in my shaking hands, but luckily didn't fall. Andy murmured, "Got a bad conscience, lovey? Young for a boy yet, ain't you? Or does the Scotch start in their cradles?"

He was smiling. I didn't need to tell him. But if I wanted to, this was the last moment I could. Later, he'd not believe me, and then ask why I hadn't told him before.

Now, or not at all.

Memories flickered like the crusie lamp flame. Master Clark – "He's a fine, romantic Prince, but I dinna see a King in him." Alastair – "The true king." Poor Dancer being led off up the path. The Duke pardoning Iain – after condemning him unjustly. Peter Falconer's white face when he came out of his cellar after hiding from the Rebels for three weeks.

And Margaret Davidson. "You'll make a king and break a king."

"I'm sorry, Alastair," I thought. And I told Andy what Aelec had told me.

Things moved fast. Andy roused Major Wolfe. As I repeated my tale to him, the master and mistress awoke and listened too, with growing frowns. The major asked two or three questions – why did the boy not tell us himself? I said he was afraid – a lie, but a white one. How did he know? He probably overheard, I said. Could he be trusted? I said he could, but Major Wolfe was doubtful.

It was the mistress who made up his mind for him. "Jeannie did a good turn for the gipsies a year or two back," she explained. "They owe her a great deal. Aye, ye can trust the lad's word."

The major had his horse saddled, and rode out in a hurry, leaving me to explain myself and my actions. But the mistress drew the master away. "Get to your bed, Jeannie," she said firmly. "No, Patrick, leave it. There's no harm done. We'll see about it the morn. We all need our sleep."

Sleep? Not me.

A while later, at two o'clock in the sleety, pitch-black morning, I heard the rattle of the side-drums and the trumpets and fifes sounding the morning call, reveille – three hours early. We learned later that the major had failed to convince the orderly officer in charge of the camp that an attack was coming, and had ordered the camp roused on his own responsibility. He was near arrested before they found out his warning was the truth.

The Prince's men, delayed by exhaustion and hunger, were debating whether to go on or abandon the attack. Then they heard, as we did, the drums and fifes, and decided to retreat. Some of them were so tired, they just wrapped themselves in their plaids and slept for all the next day – right through the battle. Others, hearing there was to be no attack, went off to search for food, and missed the battle that way.

If I had kept my mouth shut, the attack would probably have gone ahead. It might have succeeded. And Prince Charles, encouraged by this success, could have fought on, and won his war.

But I told the gipsy's news, and he didn't.

How much more of Margaret Davidson's words were true?

AFTER
THE BATTLE

I don't want to tell about the battle of Culloden, but I suppose I must. It was dreadful. The Highlanders were half of them away, seeking food or sleeping, and the flatness of the battle field meant they were slaughtered, first by the cannon, and then, after their charges had been broken by the musket fire, by the bayonets and cavalry of the redcoats.

To make it even worse than other battles, the Duke of Cumberland had given an order, against all military custom, they said; no quarter. No mercy to be shown. No prisoners to be taken, no man spared. And it was obeyed. The wounded were killed where they lay, or where they ran. And then the killing spread. Folk watching the battle, even folk who had been nowhere near the battle were killed in their homes and fields, because they were Scottish. Women and children and babes in arms, even.

It seemed to me that the redcoats were quiet enough men while they were in Nairn; but battle takes men in strange ways. They might simply have been afraid, and trying to hide it. Or they may not have seen the Highlanders as human beings. Or they may not have cared. Or maybe they just followed their orders. Some said it started when an Army surgeon, a great favourite with the men, was killed by a rebel he'd stopped to help, but no-one knew for sure. Whatever the reason, the redcoats killed and killed, until they were soaked knee-deep with blood. They killed all along the road to Inverness, and in the town, and in the countryside around. They killed and killed and killed.

And they put a guard round the battle-field for three days, to kill any wounded man that survived the freezing cold and tried to escape.

Henny ran away with his friends, to watch the battle. He came back that afternoon gabbling the most terrible stories. I couldn't bear them.

I spent the morning in disgrace, for letting Aelec in. Even though the master and mistress approved of my warning the redcoats, they disapproved of the way I had got the news. I had a painful interview with the mistress, and then worked away, but no-one spoke to me. That suited me, for I was in no mood for speech. I was already wondering if I had done the right thing. I did so more and more as the news came in, and later as the days passed and the Duke of Cumberland earned his nickname of 'The Butcher'.

All the time, I was thinking, 'Alistair, be safe! Alistair, come home safe!' In the morning, while we heard the guns thudding, and later, when the guns had stopped, I could think of nothing else. It was queer, the way I had been so taken with the lad. I wasn't worried about Major Wolfe, though he had tried to help Iain. I couldn't understand it.

It was a long, long day.

About noon, the first of the wounded was brought in to our stable, from one of the regiments off the ships. Iain had been moved down to dad's house in the morning, we had plenty leeches, and the womenfolk of the town had torn up old cloths and rolled them for bandages, so we were ready. From then on, Hugh and I were helping the master all day. The mistress couldn't stand illness or blood, a queer thing, and the master found me quick and useful. He even grew friendly to me again.

There was a steady trickle of hurt men coming in, helped along by their less wounded friends, and we were busy till near dark. Most were slash wounds, from the broadswords of the Highlanders, and not a few had lost hands and arms, but there were some who had bullet wounds, too. It was strange how deft the master's huge fingers were with a tiny probe, finding and easing out the shot. However, there weren't very many hurt on the King's side, and most of those, of course, were seen to by their own surgeons. We were finished the most by seven o'clock, and could leave Hugh to watch the men while we went in to eat.

Amanda wondered delicately that the dreadful wounds I had seen had not put me off my food; but nothing ever did that. My heart was sore for the wounded Highlanders left lying on the battlefield, but there was nothing I could do for them. I hoped Alistair was not among them.

Over the next two days I asked about him from everyone who was at the battle, but heard nothing. Though the town was reeling with triumphant King's men, I slipped down to see to Iain as often as I could. He began to recognise us, and started to talk again, in a sore whisper.

The third day, Isaac came running to the door just after sunset. I was needed at home – my dad had taken a bad turn. The mistress let me go rather reluctantly, saying I should stay the night, and not be coming up the road in the dark. "For I'd not have any lass I'm responsible for, wandering the streets these nights, with the broken Hielanders an' the redcoats about," she said. I agreed, gladly.

But as we ran down the road, Isaac told me there was nothing wrong with dad. "It's that loon as paid for Dancer, Jeannie," he panted. My chest suddenly began to hurt. "He was brought to the door wi' a Hielander, on a garron. He's hurted bad. Mam said you might maybe ken better how to help him."

There was no question in his mind about whether we should help or not. Gran, however, was of a different mind. As we entered, she was quavering, "We'll a' be hanged! We must tell the redcoats – "

"We'll dae nae such thing, mother," mam snapped.

A tall, thin figure sat by the fire, and Alistair lay on the hearth mat. "It's a risk you're taking, mistress," the thin man said. I knew him – it was Father Malcolm. A Papist in the house! Did gran know? He was in ordinary clothes now. It seemed she didn't.

"We must help him, mam," I said. My stomach was heaving. Iain, holding to the stable door-post, nodded and sighed, "Aye." Mam looked at me hard.

"Are ye mad, Jeannie Main?" demanded gran. Ellen was sniftering and wringing her hands behind her. "They're Rebels. If ye help him, ye'll hang alongside o' him. I'll hae nae part in sic madness."

"Then ye'll just hae tae leave the house, mother, an' go live wi' James," said my mam. Gran was silenced; she hated Aunt Ellen. "The lad's important tae ye, Jeannie?" mam asked. I nodded, choking.

"Why?" demanded dad.

"He's my friend," I said. What else could I say?

"We'll dae what we can," mam decided, looking at dad for agreement. As he nodded, and gran squawked in disgust and anger, she turned her attention to the figure lying at the fire.

"Isaac," said dad, "stan' at the door an' warn us if anybody comes by. Johnnie, see to the man's garron. Ellen, get some soup heated – an' stop your snivellin' an' nonsense." Ellen flounced about to heat the soup, while mam and I saw to Alistair.

"Thanks to you, Ellen," said Father Malcolm, with a smile as his bowl of broth was splashed down to him. She just tightened her lips sulkily. "We've had nothin' to eat for three days," he went on, supping fast at it. "And little sleep. I couldn't even tell you for sure how we escaped the sentries."

"Never mind now," said mam. "Just eat up, and rest yoursel'. Mind his shoulder there, Jeannie, dinna twist him. Ellen, get us more hot water. This coat'll hae tae be burned."

Alistair had been shot in the leg and the side, and bayoneted in the back, and the fine green coat and the linen I'd washed for him were black and red with blood. We had to cut and soak the cloth off him. All the work I'd done with Master Clark these last days stood well with me, as I could show mam how to deal with bullet wounds, which were beyond her experience. Luckily both balls had gone straight through, and we didn't have to try probing for them. But the wounds were bad, bad, and he'd lost a lot of blood. Lucky again, the cold had slowed the bleeding. I never thought to be glad of frost.

It took us over an hour to get him cleaned up and the wounds bandaged with moss and herbs. Iain burned his coat and all the blood-stained linen, and we hoped nobody would smell the stink. I hid his silver buttons in the fireplace. There was less money behind the stone now, but my own silver earrings were still there. Alistair, fortunately, was unconscious all the time we were dealing with him and pushing him about, but as we finished he started muttering and moaning. Mam rubbed her ear worriedly.

"God will bless you for your help to us this night, mistress," Father Malcolm murmured softly. The soup had brought a touch of colour to his face.

"I hope so, indeed," dad returned. "I hope He keeps the redcoats fae findin' ye here, tae."

"I'll be away in a short while, Master Main," the priest said. "I cannot stay here an' let you be in danger for me when I can avoid it. An' you can be sure I'll not tell who helped me, if I'm caught."

"That's a' very well," said dad, "but what about the lad there? He'll no' can go wi' ye. He canna walk for a month yet. What about him?"

"Can he no' stay, dad? Please?" I begged. "We can hide him in the stable, under the hay, an' naebody'll ken."

"That's the first place they'd look, Jean," said the priest. "No, he can't walk or ride yet. I don't know what would be the best. I have a little money -"

Mam rose to her feet. "You keep your siller," she said

sternly. "Ye'll need your money your ain sel'. We owe the lad help, an' we'll gie it freely. He'll bide here. It's our Christian duty," she stopped gran's protests, "an' we'll no' fail in it. An' we'll find a better place to hide him. Now, what about you? Ye'll need fresh clothes. Here."

To my amazement she pulled out the bundle of dad's clothes that she'd fought to stop the Highlanders taking, and sorted out shirt, breeches and a coat. Dad said nothing, though he breathed heavy. "That's a' we hae that might fit you," she said.

"You're more than generous, mistress," the priest murmured. "After what Alistair told me the Chisholms did—"

"That's by. Get intae these, now, and you can sleep here till dawn. Dear God, it's no' that long now. Bed down in the stable when ye're ready. Isaac, Ellen, aff to your beds. Jean, Johnnie, gie me a han'."

Mam opened the doors of the big box bed, and we hauled out the mattress. Under it were the spare blankets. We took them out too, and got down to the framework of wood and rope that held up the mattress. It surprised us to find that we could pull up the network of rope and its wooden frame in one piece, to uncover quite a large space at the back, underneath the bed. Mam told us to take one of the chaff mattresses down and lay it on the floor inside. Then we all three carefully lifted Alistair and laid him on it.

"Now, John," said mam, "ye'll be taken ill like we told the surgeon and stay in the box bed to cover him. Then if he cries out, ye'll dae the same, an' naebody'll ken it's no' you." We thought it was a fine plan.

Just as we were straightening up, the door opened, and Annie Ralph stuck her head in. How – ? Of course, mam had sent Isaac off to bed! Gran squawked in alarm.

"I'm that sorry to bother ye, Morag, but can I hae the len' o' a handfu' o' meal for the morn?" Any excuse did her for nosiness. She saw the priest hopping half-naked in front of the fire, shirt-tail flapping as he was pulling on dad's breeches, and squeaked in surprise. "I didna ken ye had a visitor. An' what are ye daein' there?" She started over to the bed. If she saw Alistair -

Mam turned smoothly between Annie and the bed, talking all the time, and drew her to the hole in the wall where the big meal-jar stood. "Aye, aye, Annie, ye're late round the night. We're just mendin' the bed rope. Ye dinna ken my cousin Angus? He's down frae Lochindorb to see the soldiers, but I'm telling him he'll hae to walk through to Inverness the morn. Angus, this is my friend Annie. Does that breeks fit you? It's as well to make use of them while they're good, Annie, is it no'? When John there gets the use o' his legs again, we'll mak' fresh for him. Here's a bowlie o' meal – is that enough? Fine, then, I'll see ye the morn." And Annie was smiled out of the house on a torrent of words before she could see any more.

"Dear God Almighty!" said dad. Iain was gasping, and Gran near weeping with fright. "She'll tell the whole fisher town."

"Let her," said mam calmly. "My cousin'll be awa' by first light. I'm thinkin' she never saw the lad. Are ye ready for your bed yet, sir?"

We turned back to the priest, and in spite of the strain – or maybe because of it – we started to laugh. He was at least eight inches taller than my dad, and built like a clothes pole. Round his middle the breeks hung baggy as empty mealsacks, and his bony knees shone below the calf buckles. His wrists stuck out from the coat sleeves, his skinny neck rose like a baby gull's out of the shirt.

"Aye, man," said dad with a gleam in his eye, "that's a fine suit. I never realised till now how well it fitted me. It's a revelation, just."

Mam's eyes lifted. "Dae ye ken, John Main," she said, "that's the first joke ye've made in near six months? Ye must be enjoyin' yoursel'."

Dad looked surprised. "D'ye ken somethin', Morag?" he replied. "I believe I am. I feel more alive than I hae done in long enough. Aye."

The priest smiled. "I'm glad some good has come of this day, then," he said mildly. Gran snorted in disgust. "I'll off to my bed now. God bless you all." He and Iain went through the partition, and we heard them bedding down in the hay, and the murmur of prayers, with a strange clicking noise.

He was away well before dawn. He refused to stay, in case he brought danger down on us. He even left us the garron, for he said he could travel near as fast without it, and hide a deal easier. We heard him splashing through the ford, and crunching up the gravel on the far side of the river. Then the sounds faded into the dark and mist. We never saw him again.

Alistair had little fever, in spite of the cold and the time it had taken to get him to help, but mam said it would be ten days anyway before he could walk. Town folk would take even longer, but he was young and healthy, and had been used to much exercise for a year or so before the battle.

We were fair worried. Gran was right; if we were caught helping a Rebel, we'd all hang. And Annie wouldn't keep her mouth shut. Had she seen Alistair and the place under the bed? We discussed it for long, and did what we could.

First thing that morning, we had Iain laid on the far side of the fire on a mattress. He was much better, and talking of going home. Mam, after some argument, realised it was better if she went to the market as usual, while I stayed instead of hurrying back to the Clarks' as I should. The fact that some of the soldiers knew I'd helped them might be worth the trouble being late back would bring me. Dad was still in the box bed, and gran baking oatcakes. John went down as usual to the boat, and Ellen took Isaac away out to gather bait. The twins were fed, and sat in their usual fire corner on a pile of nets, playing with some feathers.

Iain was trying to thank me.

"There's nae question o' thanks, Iain," I said. "I owed you. That night at the meeting -"

"Sh!" he whispered. He still did not have his full voice,

but a dry, husky croak. "Not a word! But I'm gratefu'. How did you convince them I wasna spyin'?"

"I just told them," I said, puzzled. "I kent ye'd no' dae a thing like that." As I saw his face twist into a bitter grin, I realised I'd been wrong. "You were spyin'!" I said angrily. "An' here me makin' a fool o' mysel' to save ye. Spyin' for the Rebels!"

"For the Prince," he whispered. "An' he'll be back."

"He'll be caught an' hanged," I retorted. "There's a price on his head would make his own mother gi'e him up."

"Never," came the husky whisper. "You dinna understan', Jeannie. He has the right!"

"I dinna care if he's got the right, left, an' centre -" I was starting to snap at him, when suddenly at the window Johnnie was gasping, "Duggie's no' at the boat – he must hae gone for the soldiers -"

He hadn't time to finish. The leather door bounced back, snapping one strap hinge, and the room was suddenly full of redcoats, six of them and a sergeant, shouting at us to keep still – as if we could do anything else. Then there was a hush, with only the noise of the seagulls; and in walked their officer – and Duggie Ralph.

I gripped Iain's hand like a lobster. Gran started to wail.

"What's this, then, Duggie?" said dad. He knew fine well what it was.

Duggie didn't look at him, but at the officer, who was peering about in the dimness, holding a handkerchief to his nose. "Fyeuch, what a stink of fish!" he muttered. In spite of the danger, I still could feel affronted. What else did he expect, in a fisher's house? He turned to the box bed where dad lay, the doors wide open. "In there, you said, Ralph?"

Duggie nodded. "Aye, sir, under the mattress." Annie had seen!

"Carry on, sergeant."

"What in the Lord's name are ye at?" shouted dad, but they paid no heed. Iain lay like a log, and I knelt still beside him, my heart pounding so I could scarce breathe, while the redcoats hauled dad out of the bed. They weren't gentle. They just grabbed his arms and pulled, and dad's body and legs were trailed out of the big cupboard and bumped down on the floor. As he fell, one of them tripped over him, and they landed together, dad underneath. I heard him gasp with pain.

They dragged him to one side and returned to the bed. Bayonets poised, they ripped out the mattress and the rope support. Then there was a blank pause.

"Nobody there, sir," reported the sergeant. "Only baskets."

Duggie went pure scarlet. "What?" he almost screamed. "He must be!"

The officer drew his face back from the blast of foul ale. "Well, he ain't!" he snapped.

"Me woman saw him! A rebel, hurted, hid under the bed!"

"Are you sure? She wasn't just imaginin'?"

"She wouldna dare! He was here, right enough. They've moved him, that's a'! Look round – he's hid here somewhere! Or outside in the whins!" Duggie frantically started to rake round in all the corners.

At a nod from the officer, the soldiers searched too. Three went outside; the rest quickly hunted the house. Their bayonets stabbed viciously into everything; they worked through the stable – the priest had been right, they started there – through all the piled nets and baskets and barrels, up under the hanging chimney that stuck out from the wall over the hearth, even into the mattresses on top of the box bed. I watched a thin trickle of chaff float down from one cut. It might have been blood. They went all through the house, right round Iain and me. Duggie even swung up to the rafters and started poking round in the thick heather thatch.

Gran was praying. I hoped God was paying attention.

The lieutenant stepped over to us and looked down at Iain. "Who is this?"

I had to clear my throat before I could reply. "My cousin, sir," I said. "The Duke was goin' tae hang him for a spy, but he didna. He canna speak right yet, see his neck there, but we're that gratefu', sir! We wouldna harbour a Rebel! Surgeon Clark kens that, sir, he's my master, an' Major Wolfe."

"Heard about that," he said. "Missed it. Pity. Interestin' thing to see. Three times, eh? However. Wasn't it you passed the word about the attack, too? H'm." Iain stiffened as he lay beside me, but kept quiet. The officer gazed round at the soldiers, standing idly. They'd finished. "The surgeon's maid. H'm. Not much likelihood of a Rebel in this house. Found anythin', sergeant?"

"Nossir!"

"Any sign of wounds bein' dressed?"

"Nossir!" We'd carefully burned everything.

The twins had been staring, enthralled by the bright red coats. Eddie got up, and crept over silently to touch the officer's glittering buttons. The lieutenant jumped, looked down at him in annoyance, and then smiled with his mouth, not his eyes.

"Hello, boy," he said, heartily. "You want a shilling?" He took it out of his pocket, bright and shining. Donnie came over, too. "Where's the man that was here yesterday, eh?"

"He'll no' tell you, daft loon!" snarled Duggie from above. The officer looked startled, and the sergeant angry, as they misunderstood the word. Then the lieutenant started to turn red and stutter with rage.

Eddie reached out for the shilling, but it was up out of reach. "Watch out, sir!" I called, but the officer paid me no heed. All his mind was on Duggie. I knew what would happen, and leaned forward over Iain, to shelter him. Without warning, Eddie leapt into the air, astonishingly fast. The officer staggered back as Eddie grabbed his wrist and with his uncanny strength hung on. Donnie – they aye acted together – flung himself at the man's knees, wrapped his arms and legs round them and clung like a squid. Naturally, the officer fell over, swearing. He landed soft in the nets, and tangled his spurs thoroughly as he tried to rise. His fine three-cornered hat, with its grand gold lace, fell off one way, and his lovely white wig the other, leaving his bristly scalp bare. Eddie had got what he wanted, the shilling, and both the boys were grinning and grunting over it by the fire.

The officer's words were mostly new to me. He was English, of course.

As he threshed about in the tangle of nets, his sergeant leaped forward to help him. He tripped on the mesh and fell too, bumping hard into the hanging lum and shaking it. Duggie was leaning out above them, trying to see clearly what was going on, one foot and all his weight on the top of the mantle. Down he came with a bellow in a shower of dust and dirt. The language from the three of them was something fierce.

But as Duggie fell, a huge lump of soot thumped down onto Gran's girdle and the oatcakes lying forgotten and curling there. The soot, as soot does, billowed out all over the room. Gran screeched, and up-turned the meal-jar over Duggie's head. He hauled it off, spluttering, hurled it away – a soldier caught it – and struck out at her, missing and knocking Eddie down on top of the officer's hat. Half-blinded, Duggie tripped over me, crashed down into the fire itself, and started to yell again. Both the twins joined their shrieks to the din.

The officer and his sergeant clambered to their feet and stumbled rapidly back from the screaming, swearing, black and white cloud that enveloped Duggie. Gradually, the shape of the man and boys began to appear again, blinking and spluttering from the mist. The twins ran to Gran, who hushed them.

As the officer stared at Duggie, his face changed. The purple of rage became the red of amusement. "My God!" he said. "Did you ever?"

We all looked more closely. Duggie was piebald; his

top half was more white with oatmeal than black, and his lower half was more black with soot than white, but he wasn't a normal sight. The soot and flour were streaked in bands across his face where he'd rubbed his eyes, and as he coughed and spluttered, swearing and cursing, he wasn't pretty.

The officer started to laugh. Duggie swiped sideways at Gran and the twins, but at a sign from the Englishman a soldier stopped him. Seeing the officer laughing, the sergeant joined him. The soldiers, watching the three of them, started to snigger. Duggie was too furious for sense, and hit out at the sergeant. A redcoat promptly knocked him down with the butt of a musket.

The officer straightened his face. "No damned Rebels here, sergeant, eh? Not even up the chimney, eh? You, Ralph, you be glad I don't arrest you for giving false information. I would, by God, if you'd not given me the best laugh since I came to this damned hell-hole. Get out of my sight, you rogue, and don't let me see you again."

Duggie, hawking muck from his nose and throat, headed for the door. As he opened it and the morning light streamed in, the officer caught sight of the sergeant. With a dreadful suspicion, he looked down at himself, and shouted, "Stop!" But Duggie had also seen, and ducked out the door before anyone could move.

The officer, too, was covered with soot and flour. He and his sergeant weren't quite as bad as Duggie, but – it was a small house. Their fine red coats had a strange mottled effect.

The soldiers' sniggers, now explained, stopped. Suspiciously straight-faced, they tried to brush the two men down. It didn't help. Soot does not brush – it smears. They picked up the officer's wig – now not so white – and his hat – now not so black. His face, where it wasn't black, was puce. After a long time, not having repeated himself once, he finally stopped cursing. He looked as if he was going to order the lot of us off to the Tolbooth.

Sweetly, praying hard, I said, "I'm sorry for the loons,

sir. They're no' right in the head. They dinna ken their own strength, sir. Duggie Ralph should have told ye."

It made him pause. It was true, it wasn't our fault.

"I am sorry they've been a bother to you," I said politely, and curtseyed as Mistress Clark had taught me. I got the pot of water that stood, fortunately covered, in the corner of the hearth. It was hot, and the water was nearly clean. I offered the lieutenant a cloth and mam's soap. I could see him calming a little as he washed his face, scalp and hands.

He looked bitterly at me, still angry, knowing fine that he was a sight. His coat was almost more white and black than red, in spite of – or maybe because of – the soldiers' efforts. The sergeant was no better. They looked ridiculous, but I didn't feel at all like laughing. The danger of being punished just to take the edge off the man's temper was still too near. "I'm that sorry, sir," I repeated. I didn't know what else to say.

There was a short pause. Dad had pulled himself into a more comfortable position against one wall, out of reach of the trampling feet. A sneeze came from the fire, where Iain lay. As we turned to him, he sniffed. He was covered in flour. Gran hugged the twins by the hearth.

"There's nae Rebels here, sir," I tried again. "Duggie's aye tried tae get us in trouble. It was him crippled my dad."

"That's true, sir," said dad from the side. The officer snorted. I beat the worst of the flour off his hat, and gave it, and his shilling, to him with another curtsey. He glared at me bitterly, and visibly controlled his temper.

"Right, sergeant, fall in the men outside. We'll get back. An' if you see that – that – him, arrest him!"

"Yessir!" The men stamped out, but the sergeant suddenly poked his head back in. "Sir -" he said urgently. The officer went out quickly.

I heard, for the first time, the muted sound of many people outside. Not making a din, or shouting. Just being there. I went to the door, and found the whole of the fishertown folk, three hundred strong, standing there, watching, the men at the front.

Duggie was still there, his back against the wall of the house.

The officer was no fool. Though he knew he looked like one, there wasn't even a snigger – perhaps the most ominous sign of the crowd's temper. Thesergeant muttered to him, but he answered, "No, leave him. Serve him right, eh, sergeant?" and the six men were formed up double-quick, ignoring Duggie, and marched off up the path. As they went, not a word was said.

The folk started to inch forward, their eyes on Duggie Ralph. Some were picking up stones.

Duggie looked round desperately, pressed back to the wall. He had gone too far this time, in his hatred of dad, and he knew it. The fishers would accept his brutality to Annie, his cruelty to Johnnie, and say only that he was a hard man. There was no proof that he'd hurt dad in the boat. But now he'd tried to betray one of their own folk to outsiders. They'd never forgive that.

Suddenly he started to run, off up the path behind the soldiers. No-one stopped him. He rounded the corner, a stone thumping his leg, and was lost to our sight for ever.

Annie, among the crowd, started to cry. One of the women led her home.

I went back into the house. Dad was grinning. I rolled Iain off his mattress. "They'll no' be back. You can breathe again now, Alistair," I whispered, and the mattress sighed and stretched under my hand, and sneezed again.

THE QUEST
FOR A KELPIE

That was the last happy hour I had for long enough. From then on, everything seemed to go wrong.

First, neither Iain nor Alistair would forgive me for having passed on word of the Prince's attack. Iain said little, but every time I ran away down to see him and Alistair, he would go off into the stable. Within two days, he'd slipped off home. I was sorry, but what could I say?

Alistair took his place as the half-hanged cousin. Nobody in the fisher town knew Iain well. The two lads were about the same size, with dark hair. We trimmed Alistair's hair to the scalp, saying it had to be done for a fever, and the change in his looks was enough to fool anyone. As for the weal round Iain's neck, mam put a poultice of dandelion stems on every night, and brought poor Alistair's skin up in a great swollen ring, dyed with bramble and walnut juice to the right colour.

He refused completely to talk about the battle, no matter how Johnnie and Ellen pressed him. He would play by the hour with wee Morag, helping her learn to talk. But with everyone else, especially me, he was withdrawn and silent, and not just from the pain of his wounds. He had dreadful nightmares, mam said. The only time he opened his thoughts to me, I wished he hadn't; for his cry, "Ach, Jeannie, why did ye no' let me die?" haunted me for many a day. He was a good patient; he did as he was told, ate what was put in front of him, took his medicine, lay still and silent while the dressings on his wounds were changed – at night, in case anyone saw; but he healed almost in spite of himself, it seemed, for there was no life in him.

But as he improved, dad grew worse. When the soldiers pulled him out of bed, they had hurt his back again, and he grew hot and feverish as he had been just after the accident, tossing and crying in pain. Mam dosed him with valerian, and washed him down with salty water, but the heat stayed. She was at her wits' end with worry.

Up at the Clarks' house, we were busier than ever. As the wounded men healed and left, the ship fever was spreading. The regiment from America brought it ashore with them, and soon it was reported among the townsfolk too. Typhus, they called it. The first signs were aches all over, and a dreadful headache, then sickness and a running gut, and foul and stinking breath. After a day or two, boils like the plague came out over the body. About one in three died. Master Clark was near worked off his feet.

Some of the sick from Houghton's Regiment were brought to us for care. The officers from Barrell's had left, to go to Inverness with the Duke of Cumberland, and we took in a new set. We didn't wash the sheets this time; the mistress said, "What? After two nights' use? Are you daft, Jeannie? I'm not workin' you hard enough, that's clear." So I didn't press the point. I had more than enough to do, with caring for the sick men, worrying about dad, helping mam when I could, and fretting over Alistair. Though he was much better, the wound in his side was still too bad to let him leave, and he still wouln't speak to me.

I was tired out. The mistress did the cooking, and the girls did a lot more of the work in the house than before, but she wouldn't let them near the sick men. That was all my task now, for Hugh took the fever, and though he recovered, for long he was too weak to help at all. Henny was a great surprise; when I was nursing his brother, the wee rogue took a pull at himself, and started to be a real help. The night the fever broke, and we knew Hugh would live, Henny even cried on my shoulder with happiness. I could scarce credit that it would last, but it did. He turned into a great lad.

But the atmosphere in the house was bad. Miss Amanda couldn't bear to look at me, with part guilt, part annoyance at the trouble she'd got into because of me. And Celia, strong on my side, sulked and avoided Amanda. The mistress was fair disgusted with the three of us, and snapped at us all. What with the sick men, and the master and mistress worried about the disease, and Celia and Amanda fighting each other over me, the tension in the house was fierce.

After about ten days we had seven sick officers and men in the house. One officer, a Captain Nisbet, was very bad. The master didn't think he'd live, though we did all we could.

But on the second of May, I got worse news than all. For Johnnie came to the door, saying that mam was ill.

"Is it the fever?" I asked, gripping his arm.

"I dinna ken, Jeannie," he said, shaking his head, "but she's awfu' bad."

I looked round. The mistress and master were out, and Miss Amanda was in charge of the house. "Please, miss," I begged, "can I go? They'll need me."

She looked worried herself. "We need ye too, Jeannie, with all the work," she said, but not very firmly. Celia, feeding the fire, watched her sullenly, for she feared as I did that Amanda might use this chance to pay me back.

I was just thinking that I was going, whatever Amanda decided, when she made up her mind. "Aye, Jeannie, off you go," she said. "I'll tell mama. Take down some of father's medicine as well."

As I dashed to get my plaid, Celia gave her sister a hug. "Good for you, 'Manda!" she said, smiling and sniffing together. "I'm so glad." Amanda stiffened a second, for she didn't often allow her little sister's grubby hands as close to her clean skirts, but she didn't push her off, and even looked pleased. "Don't worry about mama, she'd not keep Jeannie," Celia went on. She turned to me. "We'll see to the men, Jeannie, an' Henny'll help too."

"Don't come back till you're able, Jeannie," said Amanda. She put her arm awkwardly round Celia's shoulders and nodded to me. "Give your mama our best wishes for a speedy recovery."

"Oh, 'Manda!" sighed Celia. "Why do you aye talk like a grammar-book? Tell her we hope she's soon better, Jeannie. An' take care of yourself!" She looked up at her big sister with her usual sweet smile again, and as I ran out with Johnnie Amanda bent and kissed her. I envied them.

Alistair met us at the door. His eyes were alive, as if the emergency had awakened him. "How is she?" I asked anxiously.

"No' good, Jeannie," he said gravely. "I'm feart for her."

Mam was indeed ill. Her whole body shook and jerked under the blankets with the fever, and her breath stank. When I checked her armpits and legs, she had great boils starting to grow. She didn't know me.

Dad was in pain, but he was thinking and talking straight. "Jeannie," he was giving me my orders before I'd even got in the door, "ye'll hae to get the loon awa'." He went on talking as I attended to mam. "Ye'll tak' him up to yer granda's house by Coulmony. If ye're carefu', naebody'll see ye, an' ye'll be safe enough. It's far for him tae walk, I ken, but he's better, an' ye'll see he canna stay here. He wants tae help, but the best thing he can dae for us is leave."

"Oh, whit'll we dae? God kens whit'll come o' us. Whit about wee Donnie an' Eddie? Oh, God have mercy," poor gran was muttering to herself, fussing about mam with cold cloths in her twisted old hands.

Ellen surprised me. Just as dad was turning round to gran, the irritation clear on his tired face, Ellen put her arm round the old wife and led her to a seat. "Sit down, gran, an' I'll mak' ye a cup o' brose," she said. "Dinna ye fret about the loons. See them out the yard there, they're strong. They'll no' catch the fever. I'll see tae them." She looked over at dad and me. "You dae what ye have to, Jeannie," she said. I must have shown my astonishment, for she flushed. "Aye, on ye go. I can manage here till ye get back. Else or Annie'll gie me a hand if we need it. Dinna heed gran, we'll dae fine. I'll manage."

Dad hesitated for a second, then smiled at her. "Aye, ye will that. Ye're a good quean, Ellen. Ye're there when we need ye." She flushed even more, for she was more used to being scolded than praised, but was clearly encouraged. Dad nodded to me. "So ye can go wi' a clear mind, Jeannie. We'll can dae what we must. Ye'll tak' the lad awa' the morn."

It was hard to convince Alistair that the best he could do for us was clear himself out of the way, but once we did it, he was determined to go as soon as he could. We all knew his side was still not fully healed, and he hadn't walked more than the length of the room, but he made no mention of it.

I showed Ellen how to nurse mam, left her the medicine, and went back up the road to ask for leave for the next day. It was a wonder how the emergency had improved both Henny and Ellen!

The master said I was to go, in spite of the mistress's doubts. With Henny's help, and a couple of the recovered soldiers who were willing to stay and give a hand now – it was better than going straight back to their regiment – he could cope with the sick, he said. Mistress Janet sighed, but had to agree that I had a duty to my own folk, to get my cousin out of danger.

One thing the mistress did to help me, was go over with me to the Town House, to ask the Colonel in charge of the area for a pass to protect me going up the road. If I was caught with a sick man, it would go hard with me, but the pass stated that the man was known to the Area Commander not to be a Rebel. It was so good of her, when the master himself was under a cloud for having helped the rebel wounded, I felt right bad at deceiving her, but what else could I do?

So early the next morn, I tucked my precious bit of paper into my bodice, wrapped warm in my plaid against the mist, and ran down home before dawn. Mam was no better. She was still red with fever, and the boils on her arms and legs were huge, though not yet ripe for cutting, the way the surgeon did it . I'd seen some of the soldiers hotter and worse, and they'd lived. But she was just tired out, with the long winter's care of dad. Had she the strength to fight it off? I wanted to stay and help Ellen. I couldn't.

Johnnie had the new garron saddled, and even a half load of fish for me to take, for it was Friday. Alistair, more excited and alert than I'd seen him since he left for the battle, was also warmly clad, in breeks and shirt mam and gran had early on stitched for him out of dad's old clothes. They fitted him better than the good ones had fitted the priest, anyway, and didn't look too grand for a country lad.

"Here," said Johnnie, handing him a fine ash stick. "I cut that for ye a week past, on the chance ye'd be needin' it soon. Ye canna ride the whole way. The garron's too frisky to trust a whilie yet, Jeannie. He's no' been out this twa-three days."

"There's a bit bannock an' cheese in a cloth for ye," said Ellen. "It's no' great, but it'll keep."

"Aye, it'll keep your belly an' yer backbone frae kissin' for a day or two," said dad with a grin. There was colour in his face, and he looked well, when he lay still. When he tried to move more than a hand, you could see him wince. He beckoned me over. "Jeannie," he said, "go an' tak' a shillin' out o' the store. We' ve no' that much left, but we can spare a little for your loon."

I was both alarmed and pleased. My loon? And here me just thirteen? Well, maybe he was. I knew some girls that had wed at thirteen.

As gran said a prayer for us – she had nothing else to give, the soul – I eased the stone out of the hearth, and took out Alistair's silver buttons and a shilling from the hole. There was little left there, I could see. But there were my silver earrings. I could surely do what I wanted with them, without asking? I slid them into my pocket quickly.

Alistair hefted the stick, and looked round us all. Morag, tied into her little chair to keep her out from underfoot, gave him a big grin. She was all excited by the early stir, and waved madly, blethering to be let out. The twins were also grinning from the edge of the partition. Gran hadn't seen to them yet, to dress them. Isaac stood at the door, holding the pony's rein. "Safe journey, man," he nodded. Without a word, Alistair hugged Ellen, who squeaked, and Johnnie, who grunted and tried to dodge. He kissed gran, who clung to his wrist as if she, who hadn't wanted to take him in, now didn't want him to go. He looked down at mam, tossing and shaking on her bed, and shook his head, choking back tears.

Dad smiled. "Aye, son," he said. "She's bad. But she'll be better soon, please God. An' ye'll be safe. I ken her – it's ye she's most frettin' about. When she can understan' ye're awa', that'll ease her. Now on ye go, an' tak' good care o' yersel'. An' ye'll find a way to let us ken when ye're back hame again, eh? That'll please all o' us, no' just Jeannie there." I blushed.

Alistair turned, still with no word, and went out. I looked at dad. "A fine one you are, John Main, shamin' your daughter like that!" I said. I bent over and kissed him, as he laughed breathily. As I did so, I smelt the first heat and stink of the fever on his breath.

It was that which had made him so active and his colour so bright this morn, not just the excitement. Sick at heart, I glanced over at Ellen, to see her watching me. She nodded, and I knew that she had smelt it too. A knot, like the one when I was being examined by the minister, tightened in my chest.

"On ye go, Jeannie," said Ellen firmly. "The sooner ye're awa', the sooner ye'll be back."

It was true. I had to get Alistair away. If she could manage for the day – she was nearly ten, after all – she nodded again, and I turned away from my dad, sick with this fresh burden.

When I got outside, Johnnie and Isaac had walked Alistair and the garron a bit up the path, to let the pony kick the itches out of his legs, and I ran to catch them. I told Johnnie to get right back, for Ellen needed him, and they waved us away at the bridge. We headed off up the track, that daft garron biting and tugging at its rope.

We were both silent as we went.

Alistair was limping a bit, but not too badly. I hoped he could make the ten miles to the croft. Once out of the town, he could ride a good deal of the time, but it would still be a hard trip for one so badly wounded so recently. Oh well, there was nothing else for it. He'd just have to. But there was no need to tell him about dad, and add to his worries as to mine.

We took it easy. The fish were really an excuse. None of the other fisher wives were going up the country that week, with the good sales to be made to the army in the town, and the danger on the roads. We'd all heard of the folk killed by the soldiers just for being Scotch, and if the women knew I was going they'd think me crazy. So we went gently on our way, keeping a good look-out and stopping every mile or so for a rest.

Once the mist lifted it was a fine day, and warm when you were out of the cold wind, and the leaves were well out on the trees. Birds were at last nesting, and the air was full of song. The woods were carpeted with bluebells, and the whin, that never stopped blooming entirely, was turning the hillsides gold. But I was too miserable to care. Dad and mam were sick and might die. Dad was crippled; even if he lived, the money was running done. Gran was too old to work, Ellen too young, and the twins needed looked after. Then there were Isaac and Morag. What were we going to do?

If ever I needed a kelpie, it was now, I thought. The idea

132

was so daft I snorted a bit with a kind of bitter laughter, and Alistair looked down at me.

"What is it, Jeannie?" he asked. It was near the first civil word I'd had from him, and the first sign of interest in anything since the battle. I decided I might as well tell him. He wouldn't betray me or the gipsies, and it would take his mind off his aches for a mile or so.

Strangely, he was very interested. So interested, I even told him a little about the Society of Horsemen, with their bone and magic word, and pointed out to him the place where I'd buried the toad's body, which was just up the track from us.

"Go and see, Jeannie!" he ordered me. He was needing a rest, anyway, all grey round the mouth. I led the garron off the path among the whin bushes, helped him down, and as he sank with a sigh onto a tussock of heather in a sheltered patch I took my spoon from my pocket and dug into the earth. It was loose now, and easy. To my surprise, I found that my bit of cloth was not full of rotting flesh, as I'd expected, but was quite light and dry. Brushing off a few clinging ants, I took it over to him, and opened up the folds.

There in my hands lay a bundle of tiny white bones. They fell apart as I moved them.

Alistair smiled at me. "On you go, then," he urged. "There's a pool there. I'll no' watch."

"Ach, dinna be daft!" I said, but he insisted. It seemed oddly important to him. To humour him, I went over to the little peaty pool. He deliberately turned his head away, and feeling rather foolish I dropped the handful of bones into the dark water.

One floated.

I must have gazed at it for half a minute before I thought to pick it up. I couldn't really believe this. It was daft. And yet – the men had believed it. What should I do?

Alistair had no doubts. "Wrap it up in the cloth again, Jeannie, an' tie it roun' your neck," he told me. He pulled a few threads out of the edge of my plaid, to make a string for me. "There now, when ye fin' a kelpie ye're a' ready for it!" With a laugh, he lay back, and sighed deeply. When I looked at him again, he'd fallen asleep, with the easy sleep of the sick.

I sat and watched him for a while. We'd gone so slow, it was afternoon now, and we still had over two miles to go. He'd lasted better than I'd feared. With a quieter garron, we'd have been there long before, but this beast was awkward, shying and stopping, and having to be forced along. Not like Dancer at all. And now it was going short on one forefoot. Well, it would just have to keep going. It was eating heartily enough, at the end of the rope. It might get colic, though it wasn't hot. Serve it right.

What about this bone? A right carry-on, it was. Maggie Davidson and her Sight! But she'd been right about the shadow of the gallows. I scratched absently at the tiny bundle at my throat. Maybe—no, she couldn't be. But still—

I looked at Alistair again. He was deep asleep, sheltered from the wind and from sight by the whins. The Loch of Belivat was just up the hill behind us. Would I bother to go up? He'd be safe enough. I'd tether the pony here, and he'd know if he woke I wouldn't be long.

I needed help now. To save my parents, and the whole family. Could I turn away from any chance, however small and unlikely?

Ach, it was just havers. There wasn't really a kelpie. The minister had said so. And the priest.

Or was I just trying to think of reasons for not going? Was I just scared? A wee voice in my mind said, Go on, you coward.

Telling myself if I was wasting my time, well, I had time to waste, I tied the pony and scrambled away up the hill.

This was the place where granda had said the man met the water-bull. Here, in this wood. It was old and eerie, full of sighings and whisperings and a hushing roar as the wind tossed the pine needles high overhead. As I pushed through the fiddle-heads of the first bracken, I felt there were eyes all round, watching, unfriendly. I thought I heard voices echoing dully through the green shadows, but saw no-one.

The leaves were out now, and I couldn't see the water from the hill. Climbing over broken, fallen tree stumps and branches, rounding clumps of bramble and broom, pushing through the small birches and scrub alder that filled evey gap, I worked gradually over the hill and down the slopes towards the loch.

Without warning, as I forced through a barrier of broom bushes with my arms up to protect my face, the ground fell under my feet, too steep for me to keep my balance. I slid painfully down the small cliff in a shower of stones and old pine cones, and splashed on my back in four inches of muddy water, by a tiny beach of gravel surrounded by high rocks. Lucky, I thought, not to land on one of those, or I'd have hurt myself.

As I started to struggle to my feet, a snort and a clinking noise stilled me. My mouth open, my heart shaking me, I looked up.

Four feet from me stood a huge, black horse. The Kelpie.

THE KELPIE

I sat in the water, shocked beyond breathing, let alone moving, for an age. At last I saw that the monster was not going to eat me, or trample me to death, and I gasped and began to think straight again.

The kelpie was huge. It towered over me, a great black beast, its red nostrils flaring gently as it snuffed at me. As granda had said, it seemed quiet enough, and it was certainly fine. It was jet black, with no hair of white. It was saddled and bridled in black, with silver buckles and bit. The saddlecloth was red. A pair of plump saddlebags were strapped to the cantle, to tempt a thief to destruction, and a pair of heavy horse-pistols swung at the pommel.

It watched me, as I watched it. Its ears pricked forward and back, and it swung its head and tail to chase the flies. I could hear the swish of the long hair. All round there was stillness. The birds, the frogs, even the sound of the wind and the lapping water had died away. Nothing stirred but the kelpie.

It lost patience, and stepped delicately towards me. I backed off, inching through the dark water till my back came against a rock. Trapped, I used the stone to push myself to my feet, against the drag of my wet skirt and plaid, and waited. I was not as tall as the beast's shoulder. The kelpie merely sniffed at my chest, and nudged me with its huge nose, inviting me to mount. I knew exactly what it was thinking.

Of course I did! I had the bone!

It suddenly came to me that this was why I was here. If anyone could ride the kelpie, it was me. I certainly had the need. I had the bone and the word. Did I also have the courage?

Even as I thought it, the kelpie lifted its head and started to turn away, to escape. But I grabbed for the rein dangling in front of me, and held fast. Still pretending to be well trained, it stopped obediently.

I held it, my hands trembling, while I made ready. I wrung as much water as I could from my clothes, and hauled the back of my skirt up between my legs to tuck into my waistband and make a kind of trews. I wrapped my plaid tight round and round me, over my arms and shoulders, and tucked in the ends out of the way. I climbed up onto the rock, ready to mount. And then I stopped. Like a salmon at the foot of a fall, I waited for a sign to make me move.

Nothing happened.

It came to me that it was for me to make the choice. I could let go, and let mam and dad take their chance, and Alistair look after himself; or I could risk my very life, and save them all. What would I do?

Suddenly, without thought, like getting out of bed, I was scrambling up onto the kelpie's back and sitting, too scared to blink, waiting to be run away with. It was enormously high and wide.

The kelpie shook its head, near pulling me out of the saddle, and moved a few steps – out towards the centre of the loch. I woke up, and hauled on the reins in a panic. "Sic volo!" I whispered. "Sic volo!" a little louder. "Come up out of the water, kelpie. Please, kelpie!"

It obeyed. It turned, and with a splash, a heave and a rattle of displaced stones pulled itself up the steep bank. It stopped, and I wondered what to do now. Was this enough? Did I have to ride it away? How far? Was it just teasing me?

As it stood quietly, nibbling at leaves on a bush, just like a real horse, my heart beat slower. The stirrup straps were far too long, and very gently I twined my feet and legs through them, till my bare feet were supported on top of the stirrup irons and I felt safer. I took a deep breath, and "Sic volo!" I said again, clicking my tongue and kicking gingerly at its ribs, as I'd done on stolen rides on the master's horse. I was most encouraged when it started to walk forward, along the bank.

Suddenly there was a shrieking and howling in the bushes, and all the devil's imps came jumping out to save his creature. I saw their red skins flash through the leaves as they raced towards me, screeching wildly. The kelpie seemed as startled as I was. It spun round, leaping away up the brae, almost jerking me off. Behind us, I heard the devil's whip crack again and again as he urged his servants on. Just as something hit the plaid on my back with a heavy thud, the kelpie screamed, reared till I hit my nose on its neck, and then was bounding up among the trees, dodging and twisting through the pines. I hung on desperately, jolted from side to side, one hand tight on the saddle and the other gripping the mane.

As we crashed through the trees, a branch caught in my hair and near broke my neck before it snapped off. I could feel the twigs waving above my head still as we thundered up to the crest of the hill, and avalanched down the far side, but I hadn't a hand to pull it out. Blood from my nose spattered all over me, but I couldn't spare a second to wipe it.

I was being carried away, but at least not into the water. I yelled, "Sic volo! Stop! Stop!" again and again, but with no effect. As we raced down, out of the trees and across the moor, jumping the hillocks and hollows, I clung on grimly, knowing that if I fell among the rocks I'd be killed.

For a while I feared that the kelpie might put a foot in a hole and fall with me, but then I remembered it was a magic beast; it wouldn't do that. I was safe from that at least. Safe! That was a joke.

Down and down, twisting through the broom and whins we galloped, and turned right along the track towards Daltulich and Relugas. It was a little smoother than the open moor, but not much. The great beast leapt and charged the screes and corners that I took so gently with the garron, and I was hard put to it to stay on, but at least I could judge now when to lean or sway.

Now that I could see where we were going, after a while I found, to my surprise, that the ride was exciting, and not just terrifying. The kelpie's stride was longer and smoother, even on the rough ground, than the master's beast or our garron. It was almost like flying, as the huge shoulders bunched and kicked underneath me, carrying me so high above the rocks and heath. I was still scared, but the thrill of the speed lifted my heart, to yell with sheer high spirits. I even managed to catch up the reins that I'd dropped early on. Not that they did me much good; however hard I pulled, the enormous animal paid no attention.

Near two miles down the track, we swung off, up Shaw Brae. For the first time, as the kelpie mounted the steep slope, its speed slackened a touch, and I wondered if I could maybe stop it, but it thundered on, turning left again over the Lethen Bar and picking up speed back down towards the Belivat hills.

I was aching all over. The stirrup leathers had rubbed my thighs and calves raw. My legs were scratched and bruised from the whins and bushes we'd charged through, and my bare feet were sore from the stirrup bars. My backside – well, the less said the better. My arms were aching, my hands cut by the kelpie's tough mane, and my jerked neck stouned at each bump. At least my nose had stopped bleeding.

As I started to panic in case I was being carried back to be drowned in the loch second time round, as the kelpie reached the foot of the brae, leaped the burn and started the climb, I made one more try. "Sic volo! Stop!" I called, hauling at the reins with all my remaining force. And, faced with another steep slope, the beast at last heeded me.

Its gallop slowed to a canter, to a trot, and with a jolt or two, to a stop.

It was a question which of us was more tired. I didn't dare dismount. My legs simply wouldn't have held me. I sat dazed and gasping, enjoying just the relief from movement. The kelpie's sides were billowing as it heaved for breath, and its head hung low. For the moment, I was in no danger.

It was only then that I realised what I had done. I'd ridden the kelpie! I really had! "Oh, kelpie!" I gasped. I was panting as hard as itself. "Ye must gie me my wish! Mak' my mam and dad get better! An' see tae Alistair, too! An' the rest o' the house! That's what I want. An' ye must gie it tae me. Please!"

The kelpie lifted its head, and gave a whistling sigh. I knew it understood. I felt, in a queer way, sorry for it. Such a great beast, to be ridden by a wee quean. Its pride must be sore hurt. But I'd had to do it. And I'd done it! I had! Me, Jeannie Main! I'd ridden the Kelpie!

My heart leaping, a daft grin spreading all over my face, I turned the kelpie's head round towards where Alistair must have wakened, and be wondering where I was. It was near a mile away still, and I had to hammer the kelpie's ribs with my heels to make it move at all. I sat up on its back, exhausted and aching, leaning back to ease my bottom, but full of unspeakable happiness.

As we went along, I found myself singing. Mam and dad were sure to recover, Alistair would be safe – I hadn't a care left in the world. I was full of glory, like David after the battle with the Philistines, and I shouted my gladness and triumph to the hills. All the great psalms that I knew so well came leaping to my lips; hymns of praise and gratitude, of triumph and joy. I sang and sang, as the only way I could express how I felt.

The kelpie's ears twitched, and it shook its head. A devil's beast, it wouldn't like holy songs, of course.

We walked along the braeside, through the birches, till at

last we reached the little hollow among the whins. As we approached, I heard the garron whicker. Then I saw Alistair, and two others beside him. They turned to the kelpie's hoofbeats, and two of them stood amazed. The third came over to meet me, took the rein, and looked up at me, smiling.

"Well, now," said Margaret Davidson, "what did I tell ye?" Her plaid was fallen back from her oiled hair. She looked as triumphant as me.

"Whaur did ye get that horse?" demanded Alistair. "I've been huntin' ye a' ower the hill. Whaur've ye been? Could ye no' tell me when ye went aff?"

"Na', she couldna," snapped the gipsy wife. "She didna' ken hersel'. Come doon, lassie. Ye'll be sair, sair, I'm thinkin'."

Gratefully I slid down into her strong arms. The third person, Aelec, took the reins and led the beast off towards the bushes. "He's no' cool yet, Jeannie," he said. "I'll walk him a bittie more. How in God's name did ye ride a beast like yon?"

"You helped me," I said, wincing as I lay down on the grass. I wouldn't sit – not for choice, anyway. "Mind the meeting at Ferness?"

He whistled, and glanced at his mother. "Aye, aye, ma," he said, a note of respect, almost awe, in his voice.

She glanced sideways at him. "Ye'll maybe mind me more now, eh?" she said slyly. He turned away, and she laughed silently.

Alistair was fretting. "What hae ye done, Jeannie?"

"I've ridden the kelpie, for ye an' mam an' dad," I explained. As he shook his head, astonished, I told them what had happened. Alistair's face grew more and more strained as he listened. When I was done, he took my hand.

"But, ye silly wee lass, could ye no' see that's no' a kelpie? That's just a horse, that's a', an officer's horse! Yer deevils was just redcoats, tryin' tae catch ye!"

"An' they near did," said Maggie Davidson, suddenly. She was behind me as I lay on my side, and she pulled at the heavy plaid that was still tight wrapped round my shoulders, even after all the ride. I felt her tugging among the damp woollen folds, and she held out something on the palm of her hand.

"What's that?" I said, as Alistair drew in his breath sharply.

"It's a bullet," he said. I gaped at the little grey ball. "A musket ball. It must ha' been spent when it hit ye, Jeannie, an' was stopped by yer plaid there. It's God's mercy ye werena killed dead!"

I could scarcely take it in. I was so tired. "Ye mean I was shot at? An' it's no' the kelpie at a'?" I was near crying. All my fine endeavour a stupid mistake? My grand, glorious feeling faded away.

Margaret Davidson stood up. "Look at me!" she commanded. She towered above us, like an Old Testament prophet pictured in the master's big Bible. Bare feet wide planted, staff tall in her outstretched hand, hair gleaming in the late sun, she spoke with such sternness and solemnity that we could not but heed her.

"What ye dae depends on what ye think ye're daein'. Jeannie thought she was ridin' the kelpie, an' so she was. It was just as hard for her, as brave a thing to dare, as if it was the kelpie for true. Jeannie, ye'll get yer wish, that ye did it for, if there's any good in heaven at a'. An' ye can be sure o' that. What ye did was heroic. There's no' anither lass in Scotland would hae dared. So you, lad, dinna ye say tae her that she was wrang. She dared her life an' her immortal soul for ye. Be gratefu'. Ye've won a great prize here, without even kennin' it."

Alistair looked stunned, as well he might. I didn't quite understand, but somehow I felt better. "What do ye mean, a prize, Mistress Davidson?" I asked.

Her high head lowered, and she smiled gently down at me. "Why, the horse, lassie, to be sure. Ye didna think he could go hame on the garron, did ye? That horse will save him. It's fast an' strong, an' if he hides in the day an' travels at night he'll be hame afore he kens it. An' the ride'll be easier than walkin'."

I pushed myself up. "But my granda -" I was saying, when she interrupted me.

"He canna go tae yer granda's house. The redcoats, damn them, searched a' the crofts, an' wrecked them, Jeannie. There's naethin' there now. The house is burned – na'," as I gasped with horror, "the folk were warned, an' got awa' safe. They're a' up the hill at the summer shielin'. But the most o' the animals hae been ta'en, an' the tools an' ploughs broken. The soldiers destroyed it a'. They think a' Scotch folk is Rebels, an' the things they've done to folk that they've caught wad sicken ye tae hear o'. Your family couldna take in a stranger. He'll hae tae head for hame now, this very day. An' the horse ye've brought him will carry him easy."

I remembered how smooth the ride had been – some of it. It was true. Riding would be easier, on this animal, whether it was a kelpie or no. But –

"I'll manage, Jeannie," said Alistair. "How could I fail, after whit ye've done for me? I'll be fine. Just gie me a hand up, an' I'll ride safe."

"Aye, the beast's tired out, an' will be for a day or two," said the gipsy. She whistled, and Aelec came back with the huge horse. Now that I saw it straight, I could see that it was just a horse, tired almost to falling over its own feet. It wouldn't run away with Alistair, that was for sure.

"Look at that," said Aelec. There was a long red weal on the beast's shoulder.

"That wis a musket ball, tae," said his mother. "That'll be why he ran sae fast an' far wi' ye, Jeannie. It's a miracle ye didna fa'. Now, son, ye'd best go now, whiles there's daylight left. That soldiers will be searchin' for the beast round here, an' ye'd better be well awa'."

I knew she was right, but I didn't want to accept it. Alistair, though, saw that it was necessary. "Aye, I'll need tae gang." He rose to his feet and turned to the horse.

"My," he said, trying to lighten the moment, "would ye look at them fine saddlebags. Weel stuffed, I'll wager. The King's officers takes guid care o' theirsel's." He opened one, and peeked in. "Aye, there's a grand bit bread an' meat, an' a flask o' wine, too," he said, smiling, though his voice was wavering. "I'll be drunken, goin' down the road, eh, Jeannie?" His voice broke. He turned to me as I got up, and swallowed hard. I hugged him as desperately as I had clung to the saddle, and he hugged me back, but after a moment he put my hands bye. "Weel, goodbye, then," he muttered. He couldn't look me in the eye. Aelec led the horse in front of a tree stump, and Alistair climbed with difficulty into the saddle.

"Ye'll never manage!" I said.

"I must, my dear," he said grimly. "God be wi' ye, Jeannie – an' ye, Mistress Davidson. I'll come back, Jeannie. Some day, I'll come back. Some day soon." I couldn't answer. He pulled the horse's head round, and they walked off into the birches along the hillside. Like the time he'd left me before, he didn't look back. I couldn't even wave to him.

As he was hidden in the leaves, I cried. That was twice I'd lost him.

It was the gipsy that brought me back to life. Briskly, with no sympathy, she started sorting my plaid and skirt. "For ye're lookin' liker a tink than I am mysel'," she said as she re-plaited my hair tidily. "Now, ye're no' to fret for yer lad nor yer granda. They'll dae fine. Ye just get aff hame, an' sell yer fish on the way, if ye can find anybody wi' money to buy. Dry yer e'en, lass. Ye're a bonny sight. Yer lad would be ashamed o' ye, cryin' for what ye canna help."

As she rearranged my plaid to hide the blood from my nose, I standing like a statue, I remembered my earrings that I'd meant to give to Alistair. They were sitting uselessly in my pocket. I felt sick.

Suddenly Aelec whistled a warning, from away in the whins, but it was too late. We were surrounded by soldiers.

144

We'd been so taken up with my troubles that we'd not been paying attention. Margaret Davidson went quite white under her brown skin, and I saw that she was terrified as she'd never been in the Tolbooth. The redcoats must have done dreadful things. I shrank away from them.

Panting and bad-tempered, they grabbed the garron's rein, and our arms, and dragged us out from the whins to face their officer. He stood in the path, stout and angry, red-faced to match his red coat, a riding-whip tap-tapping at his dusty boots. Riding boots with spurs. This must be the owner of the horse.

He questioned the gipsy sharply, seeming surprised that she had the English. No, we'd seen no horse, she cried, weeping and wailing. We were poor folk. We'd done nothing, we'd seen nothing, we knew nothing. He didn't believe her.

"Hold the bitch!" he shouted, and as the soldiers held her tight he started to flog her with his riding-whip. She twisted and screeched, begging for mercy. I remembered her silence when she was whipped in the town, and the advice I'd been given about what to do if attacked. She thought there was still hope, then. I couldn't see it, myself.

The captain turned away as two more redcoats came up to report no sign of the horse. It was a small relief. While his back was turned, Margaret Davidson's earrings were dragged out of her ear, tearing the flesh, and as she wept, they laughed.

"What's that?" The captain turned back. He could stop them. He didn't. "All loot to be handed in, and shared equally!"

"Aye, sir!" the corporal answered. He was pulling at my hair, in its new plaits, and drew his knife. "Get a good price for this, lads!" he shouted, starting to hack at it. I screamed and fought, but they held me until it was all cut off.

I hoped they might let us go now, but the captain had other ideas. "Hang the pair of 'em, corporal," he snapped, "and let's get on!"

They started to drag us towards a nearby tree, and one produced a well-used rope.

In terror, I jerked nearly out of their grasp, and as they grabbed me again, my bodice tore and the pass from the Colonel, that I'd quite forgotten in my panic, fell to the ground. A soldier snatched it up with a shout of glee and handed it to the officer.

"What's this, then? Plots and treason, eh? Damned Scotchies," he snarled, opening it out. Everything stopped for a moment as he read. Then he stared at me in disbelief. "What's this, eh? Eh? Not a Rebel? Where did you steal this?"

"I didna!" I gasped. "I'm no' a Rebel! In God's name, sir, that's my pass!"

"Why not show it before, then, eh? Eh?" He struck me across the face with his whip. "Damned Scotch bitch. Why not, eh?"

"I was too scared, sir! I forgot it!"

"Lyin' bitch! Where's this cousin, then, eh? Eh? If he's not a Rebel, why is he hidin', eh? Eh?"

"He's scared too, sir!"

"Why are you off the road, eh? Look at me, you bitch. What were you up to, eh? Eh? Hidin' Rebels, eh?"

Through my terror and pain, I suddenly saw a face I knew. One of the soldiers behind the officer was a man who'd had a wounded shoulder, and I'd helped him. It was as if he was a life-line. I knew if we couldn't satisfy the officer, we'd both be killed. I just prayed that the man would recognise me, and be willing to speak up for me against his officer's temper.

"Him there, sir, he kens me! He kens I've helped the Duke's men, at after the battle! I helped sew up his arm!"

The officer spun round, his spurs caught in the heather and he staggered slightly and swore. In that second, when all eyes were on the soldier or the officer, not me, and the redcoat was looking hard at me, I stuck my hand down into the deep pocket of my skirt and pulled out my earrings. I held them in my hand, low down so that they weren't obvious, and showed them to him alone. Clearly, if he backed me up, I would give them to him. If they were found by the rest, their price would be shared among all the men. I prayed that the bribe would be sufficient to make him speak. It was my last hope. If it didn't work, it was the rope, or a bayonet, for both of us.

The officer glared at the man. "Well, Dewhurst, what d'ye say, eh? Eh? D'ye know this bitch, eh?"

The man hesitated for a year. Then he nodded. "Yessir, I does. She were the surgeon's lass. Saved my arm, sir, an' Sergeant Dicks's life, she did. An' -"

"What?" The officer wasn't pleased.

The redcoat gulped and went on. I was about to faint with tension. "Corporal Fletcher, in Barrel's, sir, he said as how it were her what give warnin' o' the night attack, sir! Acause her cousin weren't hanged, sir! Can't say meself, sir!" He was earning his silver.

The captain looked even more angry. For a moment I thought he was going to order us killed, as the simplest way out of this situation. But he didn't. He turned back to me, and snapped, "Right, you Scotch bitch!" He didn't seem to know any other word. "Where's this cousin, eh? You produce him, an' I'll credit your word. Where is he, eh? Eh?"

There was a pause. I knew that I couldn't produce my 'cousin'. I was just giving myself up for lost when Margaret Davidson spoke up. "Aye, Jeannie!" she called, louder than she needed, but then they knew she was afraid. "You call him, an' he'll come out! Sure he will, when he sees ye need him! He'll come!"

I remembered Aelec, hidden in the whins, no doubt close and listening. Now if only he'd dare to come, and risk his own life... I shouted, as loud as I could with my throat so dry, "Iain! Iain, come out! If ye dinna come, I'll be dead! Please, Iain! Iain, where are you?"

There was another pause. The officer was starting to get restive, when at last the bushes stirred, and Aelec came

147

reluctantly forward, his kerchief pulled high round his neck. He was seized and dragged to stand in front of us.

The officer inspected him carefully. "Who're you, eh? Eh?"

Aelec swallowed. He didn't have to act scared. "Iain Mackay, sir," he said in a husky voice, very like Iain's had been.

"You're the one that was half-hung, eh? Let's see, let's see!"

My heart stopped again, but Aelec stood still – he hadn't much choice – as a redcoat pulled off his kerchief. And round his neck there was a wide yellow mark, like a fading bruise, with a twisted scar in the middle of it. It was exactly like the mark left on Iain's neck.

The officer leaned over to examine it, and nodded. "You're the one. Well, I suppose I've got to take this letter for true, eh? Have you seen a horse? Damned Rebel stole it. Saw him riding off, damned feather in his hat." That must have been the branch of pine needles in my hair. I didn't want to laugh. "Big black horse. No? Well, you find it, there'll be a reward. Best damned horse I ever had. Carried me sixty miles yesterday, ready to run again today." As if I didn't know. "If I don't find it, I'll hang every Scotch bastard I lay hands on, damme if I don't. Get on, sergeant. Spread out and search the hillside."

A minute later, the three of us trembled alone in the clearing. Pass or no pass, they'd taken the garron and the fish, and our plaids, and my hair, with no thought of apology. We were only Scotch; why should they bother? At least they'd not killed us.

I'd slipped the soldier my earrings. He might have changed his mind, and said he was mistaken.

They could still return. We ran for our lives. As I ran, sore troubled about the legs, I wept for my hair and my hurt face. Aelec was laughing. His mother was cursing blackly, for her back was sore, her ear torn and her earrings gone, like mine. But we were all glad to be alive.

A mile down the road, we stopped. When we'd recovered a bit, Margaret Davidson spoke to me seriously. "We part here, Jean Main," she said. "Ye'll be safe home. Have faith, lass. Have I ever told ye a thing that's no' true? Did I no' say it? Four times linked in the shadow o' death? Choose a king, an' ride the kelpie? Aye, we were in God's hand this while past. Ye'll have yer wish. On ye go, now." She gave me a smile, and her voice changed again. "Aelec! I'll hae to get on tae reach the camp afore night. See can ye no' get us a rabbit or a pigeon for the pot ere ye come in. God keep ye, Jeannie!" She walked off into the trees, and disappeared among the leaves.

Aelec nodded to me, and was turning to go when I stopped him. "Aelec! How did ye–" I pointed to his neck.

"Whin blossom an' tobacco juice," he said with his sly grin. "Mam did it yestre'en."

"How did she ken?"

"How does she ever ken? She's wise. I'll see ye next year." And he was gone too.

It was dark before I got home. As I pushed open the door, I could hear gran praying. Mam's pallet was still and quiet. My heart near stopped.

Ellen held up the crusie, her face warm and smiling as the sunrise. "Look, Jeannie!" she said. I looked again. Mam was sleeping peacefully. The fever had broken. She would get well.

But Ellen pulled me over to the bed, where dad was tossing and twisting with pain and heat. "See there!" she whispered. And under the blanket, at the foot of the bed, just the least little bit, dad's feet were kicking.

God bless that kelpie.

Epilogue

And so, my dear Celia, I come towards the end of this story.

It was weeks before dad could stand and walk properly again, and he was never quite as strong in the legs as he had been, but he was fit to take his place in the boat by the end of the year. Donald's brother-in-law came in to make the fourth, and Johnnie could leave the fishing and get back to his books.

But before that, I was back home again, for good, it seemed. For the master, Patrick Clark, that fine, gentle big man who had worked more than anyone with the sick, at last took the fever himself. I went back up to help, but it was too late. The young officer, Captain Nisbet, died on the 14th of the month, and the master the next day. They were buried together, in the same grave.

The mistress took it hard, and blamed me. For if I had not gone off, she said, he might never have been smitten, or might have been less tired and more fit to live. Her feeling, I suppose, was only natural. Miss Amanda, to do her credit, stood out for me, and Celia wept sore, but I was dismissed. I wept too.

It was a hard summer for me, with the news coming and coming of the terrible ways that the Duke of Cumberland and his soldiers earned his dreadful nickname. I often wondered if I'd made the right decision, the night of the attack. But who was to say that if the Chevalier had won that night, there might not have been worse fighting, with more men killed, and Scotland even worse off at the last of it? God alone knows.

The minister, Alexander Rose, came to a bad end, God forgive him. He left the town and his wife, and tried to make his fortune dealing in the cattle taken from the Highlands by the King's men. But all his cows died on him, at the croft he left them at; I heard all the crofts round about didn't have a single cow die that year, but all the minister's did, it was quite remarkable. The farmer did well, but Master Rose was ruined. Nobody I knew wept for him.

In the back-end of the year I watched and waited, and passed the time slowly, nursing gran, who was failing, and the twins. I started to teach Isaac and Ellen, and some of the other fisher children, to read and write, as I'd been taught. Then word came that Alistair had reached home safe.

It wasn't until I got the news that I knew how I'd worried. Foolish that I was, I'd had in my mind that the kelpie might only give me part of my wish. I started to sing and whistle again, as I'd not done for long. Mam and dad looked sideways at me, but said nothing. Gran said plenty.

The next year, when I was fourteen years old, Alistair came for me. There was never another loon for me, since that night I'd sewed his breeches for him.

In time, we set up business in Edinburgh, and prospered enormously. I was, for a time, the wife of a Member of the Council; Alistair's father had managed to gloss over his son's connection with the Rebellion until it became a fashionable thing to have done. I sometimes wonder how Mistress Rose knew, if she really had a touch of the Sight. I met her again in Edinburgh, and found she'd forgiven me. And I met dear Celia. Five years later, she was married on a lawyer. No, not my brother Johnnie, but a friend of his.

I had six children that lived, and you, my dear, are descended from my eldest daughter.

So now, my little great-great-granddaughter, you know all my story. How you got your name, how I, a barefoot fisher girl, turned the history of the Kingdoms of England and Scotland to my choice, and how, most important of all to me, how I rode the Kelpie. Writing it for you has brought it back to me so vividly, that I can see and smell again the hot breath of the beast on my face, and feel my heart leap again in my breast at the glory of the ride. He drew the carriage for my wedding, when I first wore the pearls I am leaving to you. Poor, unmagicked kelpie! I loved him and treasured him always.

Do you love and treasure my pearls also, and remember the hard pains I had to win them.

Your loving great-great-grandmother,

Jeannie Main Gillies

AUTHOR'S NOTE

Jeannie Main and her family are imaginary, but there are many of their name in Nairn still. I have used real Fishertown names for all my Fisher folk and must apologise to the Ralph family for making one of them the villain.

Many of the people in this story really existed. Patrick Clark was the surgeon and Depute Sheriff of the time, and did condemn Margaret Davidson, a gipsy, to the punishment described. His wife was a daughter of Rose of Broadley, a Jacobite sympathiser. He died as I have said, and was buried with Captain Nisbet, one of the last victims of the typhus epidemic.

The story of Minister Alexander Rose Macinucater is told in 'Culloden' by John Prebble, to which I owe an enormous debt for information. I changed the name to Macnaughten because I felt it was more likely; I felt that the 'gh' in Macnaughten could well have been sounded at that period, and, given that supposition, if you try writing it fast, you will see how an Englishman, re-reading after some years the rough diary jottings of a half-heard, half-understood foreign name, could mistake the spelling.

I also owe many thanks to my many friends for their information and help, and to my husband, who has uncomplainingly put up with (enjoyed?) my absence in the evenings for so many weeks.

I have tried to be accurate and true to the spirit of the times in this story, without going too deeply into the horrors, filth and casual brutality which we nowadays find it almost impossible to imagine in this country. It is, after all, a story for children. I hope they find it interesting, and like reading about Jeannie Main as much as I did writing about her.

GLOSSARY

a' — all

adze — tool for shaping wood, like an axe with its head on sideways

again them a' — against everybody

ane — one

awa' — away

aye — always

Bailie — Town Councillor

bane — bone

ben the hoose — in the far end of the cottage

brogans — skin moccasins

ca' — call

ceilidh — (Gaelic) party

creel — basket for carrying fish on the back like a rucksack

dae — do

daffing — joking

dour — unemotional

garron — sturdy pony

girn — whine, cry

grieve — farm manager

hae — have

Hielan' — Highland

Hielan's — Highlands, Highlanders

hingin' — hanging

illchancy — unlucky

jappled — sloshed about

jougs — metal headcollar to chain wrong-doer to wall, like a pillory

ken — know

laldy — trouble, scolding, birching

loon — boy

lossin' — losing

lug — ear

mair — more

midden — rubbish heap round houses

mo chridh — (Gaelic) my dear

ower — over, too much

philabegs — kilt and plaid

quean — girl

reiver — raider, especially for cattle

sic — such

shift — petticoat with sleeves

skilly — skilful

starvin' — dying (not always of hunger)

stouned — throbbed with pain

syne — since

thrawn — stubborn

trock — rubbish

wee — small